DEXTER'S
Renaissance

LEE NORTH

Hot Romance Erotica

WARNING

This book contains sexually explicit scenes and adult language. It may be considered offensive to some readers. This book is for sale to adults ONLY.

* * * * * * * * * * * * * * * * * * *

Please store your files wisely where they cannot be accessed by underage readers.

Please feel free to send me an email. Just know that these emails are filtered by my publisher. Good news is always welcome.

Lee North - **lee_north@awesomeauthors.org**

About the Publisher

4Fun Publishing, a member of **BLVNP Incorporated**, 340 S. Lemon #6200, Walnut CA 91789, info@blvnp.com / legal@blvnp.com

NOTE: Due to the highly emotional reaction of some people to works of erotic fiction, any email sent to the above address that contains foul language or religious references is automatically deleted by our anti-spam software and will not be seen. All other communications are welcome.

DISCLAIMER

Please don't be stupid and kill yourself. This book is a work of FICTION. Do not try any new sexual practice that you find in this book. It is fiction and not to be confused with reality. Neither the author nor the publisher or its associates assume any responsibility for any loss, injury, death or legal consequences resulting from acting on the contents in this book. Every character in this book is over 18 years of age. The author's opinions are not to be construed as the opinions of the publisher. The material in this book is for entertainment purposes ONLY. Enjoy.

Dexter's Renaissance
Hot Romance Erotica

By: Lee North

© Lee North 2014
ISBN: 978-1-68030-018-5

Chapter 1
Discovery

There is something to be said for living in a tropical paradise. First, there's the sunshine. Second, the year round warmth. Third, the scantily dressed women.

Yes indeed, it can help restore the emotional balance of a wounded man. But that day, it was simply hot. I had only just arrived on this island two weeks earlier and I wasn't quite prepared for continuous heat. To me, hot usually means beer, and around here, beer means Grolsch ... or Heineken ... or in a pinch, Amstel.

Those are the deep thoughts that passed by me as I lounged on the balcony of my little room in Cole Bay, Sint Maarten, just a tiny speck of land in the eastern Caribbean that almost totally relies on tourism. It's a shared island, part Dutch and part French. The French have the biggest territory, St. Martin, but more people live here in Sint Maarten, the Dutch territory.

From my balcony you can see St. Kitts, St. Bartholemey, Antigua, and a couple of other islands with the naked eye. My little abode sits on a strip of land with the Caribbean on one side, Simpson's Bay Lagoon on the other, and the airport too damn close.

This was my chosen residence. Just me, myself, and I ... Dexter McLeod. Age: forty-seven, height: six-foot-one, weight: one-ninety, eyes: blue, hair: blonde-grey, skin: gradually turning brown, status: separated. I was enjoying my exile, along with the seventy five thousand fellow island residents and god knows how many cruise ship tourists.

Not so many days ago, I was the head of the CADD department at Pinecone Engineering, a medium sized firm in Vancouver, British Columbia. Twenty-three years earlier, when computer aided design was in its infancy, I was one of their first hires to effect the conversion. Fresh out of technical college, they needed someone to begin the move from old-style drafting to computer design and modeling.

I had pretty much created the department myself, so that made me Pinecone's Computer Aided Design and Drafting guru.

It was a good job and I was well paid. I was home every night except when I had to travel to a jobsite, but that wasn't very often. I had twenty-six designers reporting to me and I got along well with all of them. The tech schools were turning out a lot more young people with the necessary skills, so we could be picky about whom we hired. However, in the end, experience was a big benefit and that's what I had in spades.

With my wife, Sandra, and our two children, Jonathan, 22, and Meredith, 20, we lived in a nice suburban two-storey house only a few blocks from the commuter train station. We lived in Maple Ridge, east of the city of Vancouver, British Columbia. I would get up at five AM and catch the five-forty-five train to the city, giving me almost an hour to enjoy a large latté and the morning paper. I'd leave the office at four and be home by five-fifteen. Other than the early rise, it was quite a satisfactory routine.

Sandra's a good-looking woman. I know a hundred guys who would love to have her, but she chose me. She was five-six, a hundred thirty pounds, with a nice body that she'd kept through two kids. Dark brown wavy hair, cut at the base of the neck, brown eyes, a button nose, and perfect teeth to show off a great smile. All things considered, I felt I was a pretty lucky guy to have found her.

Sandra hadn't worked during the children's early years but got bored with being alone at home when they were in their teens. She looked around for a part-time job, but with her limited skills, it wasn't easy to find one. Then luck, or fate, took over.

Our financial advisor, Randall Teller, was visiting our home one evening and in general conversation, mentioned that he needed someone to help him with organization at his office. Simple work really: filing, taking messages, organizing meetings.

It wasn't a full time job and it didn't pay much but he was looking for someone just like Sandra. You can guess the rest. She jumped at the chance and started the next week. I didn't mind. She would start at one in the afternoon and come home at five. That gave her the entire morning for any housework or meal preparation.

Occasionally, she would help Randall with organizing a seminar for clients and prospects. They were usually held either at ten in the morning or seven in the evening at one of the local hotels. They were only held once every three months, so I didn't notice much change in our routine. I certainly had no complaints.

Things gradually changed as the kids finished high school and started their post-secondary educations. Jonathan, now called Jon, had decided on an engineering degree. At first, he thought he would take Environmental Engineering but ultimately decided on Mining and Mineral Processing. I think both Sandra and I were completely baffled by his choice. Talk about a reversal of thinking!

Meredith, Merry to most of us, had chosen interior design and had been attending two years of community arts school. She had an eye for colour and design and both Sandra and I thought she had made a good choice.

Jon would now be in his final year and Merry would be finished with her training and out looking for a job at the end of her current semester. We had corresponded briefly by e-mail but it was pretty unsatisfactory since most of the e-mails were either dumping on me or begging me to come back. That wasn't going to happen.

So how did I get from there to here? Simple. I discovered my wife was having an affair with good old Randall and planned to divorce me. She would get at least half of everything I had worked for over the past twenty-three years and I thought that was completely unfair. So, I took action.

I had very little leverage over my assets. Obstacle number one: I had originally bought our home in joint ownership with Sandra. To sell it or even re-mortgage it would require her signature as well as mine. Obstacle number two: I had set up separate RRSP's (Registered Retirement Savings Plans) for Sandra and myself. Mine was worth close to $400k while Sandra's was a little over $200k. In a divorce, she would get at least $100k of mine. Since she was having the affair with Randall, cashing in my RRSP or even moving it to another firm would immediately send up a red flag and alert them that I was onto their plans.

I could easily empty the chequing and savings accounts and cash in a number of old whole life insurance policies I owned in my name. The two term policies had little if any cash value, so I would simply change the beneficiary on them to the children. I would also change my will.

I thought about trying to trick Sandra on the mortgage. It was up for renewal in the next few months and I wondered if I could set it up so that she would sign the papers without really noticing that I was the sole title on the document. It was a small mortgage, one hundred thousand on a house recently valued at six hundred thousand.

I discarded that idea. The house itself was titled in both our names. In addition, I was pretty sure that her lover would want to see anything that might involve their plan to take advantage of me and he would spot that strategy right away. Again, that might also tell them that I was on to them and force them to change their plans.

I also learned they were willing to wait for my twenty-fifth anniversary at Pinecone. In seventeen months, I would be receiving a nice contribution that I would add to my RRSP and they didn't want to miss out on that. It was a very tidy package of stock that would be worth a great deal when I decided to retire. Unfortunately, through my ignorance, Randall was made well aware of this future windfall during our discussions about our financial affairs. They were willing to wait to make sure they would get the stock included in the property settlement as a lovely parting gift.

I was convinced Randall was the mastermind behind this scheme. Sandra wasn't stupid but she wasn't that wise to the ways of finance. She apparently had dreams of wealth and leisure and Randall would make them all come true.

Randall had sired five children, currently all between the ages twelve and twenty. He was fifty-something years old and normally would have to work hard for some years before he could retire and take it easy. His wife, Laura, was an unattractive woman in her early forties who spent most of her time looking after the five children. They had decided to home-school them and that was her role on top of looking after the household. A full time job, for sure. I wondered what she would think of this plot. The courts would not be kind to Randall leaving her and running off with another woman.

I suppose you're wondering how I found out about my wife and her lover. Well, like most of these things, it was accidental. Both Sandra and I had laptop computers. I needed a laptop for my road trips and Sandra wanted one for her job. I had set up a wireless system for the house and bought a laser printer with wireless capability that either of us could access.

Sandra isn't particularly gifted when it comes to computers. It took me hours to help her create even the simplest Excel templates and then get her to understand how to use them. Hardly a week would go by when she wouldn't summon me to help her untangle some problem or other that she'd created. I guess I shouldn't be too critical. I was using a computer all day, every day. It was a matter of the experience that I had and she didn't.

In self-defence, I created a network where I could get into her computer from mine. That way I could see what she was doing without having to stop everything and sit on her system and patiently explain what she had done wrong and what I was doing to fix it. I didn't bother to mention this to her. I didn't think it was important at the time.

Sandra discovered e-mail early on. She thought it was wonderful and was happily adding to her mailing list of friends and family on a regular basis. I would pass along the occasional joke or funny video that was sent to me by my friends. She would keep everything. Luckily, she had lots of capacity on her hard drive since, aside from the videos and family photos, nothing else took up much space.

One Sunday afternoon, I walked into her "sewing room" where she kept her computer. She had been on it for some time and I was about to ask her if she would like me to get some Chinese take-out for dinner that night. She jumped when I appeared and quickly closed the lid on her laptop, pretending to have finished with it. She stood up, but the look on her face told me that she'd been caught at something she didn't want me to see.

She quickly agreed to my suggestion about the Chinese food and pulled out the menu from the local restaurant and chose some items. I nodded and took the menu with the discount coupon and stuck it in my shirt pocket. But I was curious. What had she been looking at that caused her to react the way she did? It was easy enough to find out.

I went back downstairs to my home-office in the basement and logged onto her computer. The thought crossed my mind that she might have been surfing porn sites. That would be interesting. Let's just have a look. Nope. She was on her e-mail program. I wouldn't normally look through her mail but her reaction to my surprising her got me more than a bit curious.

I looked in the sent file and saw several messages that she hadn't filed yet. I clicked on the one she had just written and began to read. That's when my nice little world turned to shit.

Randall, my love. When is our next seminar? I can't wait to have you inside me again. That wonderful feeling of being so filled and satisfied is impossible to forget. Soon, please Randall. Having sex in your office is too dangerous.

I don't know if I can wait another seventeen months until we can be together forever. I need you more than just once a week.

Please, help me. I love you,

Sandra

I don't know how you would feel reading something like this from your wife, but I was devastated. It was so completely out of the blue that I had no warning or preparation for it. We had been married just after I started at Pinecone and for the entire twenty-three years I believed she was the love of my life and I was the love of hers. Now ... it appeared that I was about to be replaced.

My stomach was in a knot and I could hardly breathe. My head was spinning and I thought I might pass out. I sat staring at the screen -- I don't know how long -- seeing nothing but those destructive words. I was frozen in place, not knowing what to do. Could I stop this? Could I win her back? Maybe it was just a fantasy letter that her imagination had created. I was immobile with shock.

I'm not certain when I came back to the land of the living. It was several minutes I'm sure. My only thought was to see if this was just an overactive imagination ... perhaps something my wife was acting out in private. But ... she had sent the e-mail. She had sent it to Randall. I put my hand back on the mouse and began to explore.

It took me a while to find the subfolder where she foolishly kept her personal e-mail. It was hidden under "Family," which I found quite offensive. I opened a subfolder marked "Nineteen Eleven" and found at least fifty e-mails, all of them to or from Randall Teller. Nineteen Eleven? What did that mean? Then I had a thought that ran chills through me. Nineteen Eleven; the nineteenth of November. My anniversary date at Pinecone.

In one year and one hundred-and-fifty-five days, I would celebrate twenty-five years with my employer. Yeah, I was keeping track. Why wouldn't I? On that day I would receive twenty-five hundred shares of Pinecone stock. I had been getting some stock options over the years and they were the foundation of our Registered Retirement Savings Plans. Aside from the two originating partners, I was one of only three people who'd been around that long. It was a more than generous reward for loyalty. Current value on today's market: $100k, give or take. Future Value: As much as $250k if the rumour was true. More again if I held on to them for any length of time.

The rumour being quietly circulated in the office was that a very large international firm wanted buy us out and was willing to pay a big number to get us. I hadn't shared this with Sandra as I didn't want to get her hopes up. I wasn't sure that Randall might not have picked up on the rumour however. He was constantly watching the stock market reports.

I read through several of the more recent e-mails. There it was in black and white. The plan was to work me until my anniversary date then dump me for everything she could get from me. Cold blooded you think? Yeah. Ice cold! I wondered as I ran a copy of every e-mail to the printer on my desk. When did she stop loving me? I know there was a time when I never had a doubt about her but that's over now. When did it end?

She'd been working for Randall Teller for over three years. I can't imagine it was going on before then. She hardly knew him. So it had to start later on. Her e-mails dated back a little over two years and at first they weren't at all personal. That began a little over eighteen months ago. From then on things got more intimate and inappropriate with each succeeding one.

Teller was in his early fifties, ten years older than Sandra. He was a little shorter than me but seemed to be pretty fit. Styled grey hair and nice business clothes made him look very much like the successful professional. Until now I never had any reason to dislike Randall, but that had all changed in a heartbeat. He was intent on stealing my wife and a good part of my hard won wealth. I was obligated to defend myself and I would do that any way I could, fair means or foul.

The company that Teller represented was an internationally known investment firm with offices throughout North America and Europe. I decided that one of my many projects over the next little while was to satisfy myself that Mr. Randall Teller hadn't been tampering with my accounts, specifically with my RRSP. I no longer cared what he did with Sandra's but I would guard mine with my life. I would be going over my statements for the past two years very carefully.

Chapter 2
Planning

I'm a computer guy as I've already explained. But once in a while, when I'm faced with a problem that isn't easy to solve, I revert to pen and paper. I was determined to develop a plan that would allow me to extract every last dime I could from my modest wealth. I was going to need it in my new life, whatever that would be.

So I began to make a list of things.

Date: Mar. 25/07

> *Home Equity: ± $500k*
> *Home Value: ± $600k*
> *Debt: $100k Mortgage Term: expires 31/5/07*
> *Problem: Joint ownership*

> *RRSP: DMcL ±$400k*
>   *SMcL ±$200k Not available*

> *Savings:*   *Joint account $5k prox.*
> *Chequing:*   *Joint account $3k – 5k prox.*
> *Business:*   *DMcL work account $2k prox.*

> *Stock: Future -- 2500 shares Pinecone stock @ $40/share current value Protect! through 19/11/09*

> *Obstacles:*   *Cost of Divorce – lawyer's fees (both?)*
> *Divorce Law ... 50% split all assets ... plus Alimony?*
> *No Divorce Option - Disappear?*
> *Other Options?*
> *Joint Ownership on house*
> *Early warning may prompt them to act sooner than 19/11/09*
> *Who to trust?*

The more I thought about it, the more appealing just abandoning the marriage looked. But that would require a very different strategy. If I could find a way to protect more of my assets, it would put the ball in my loving wife's court.

In a perfect world, I would re-mortgage the house to the hilt and pocket the cash. Since the mortgage was paid by monthly direct transfer, it would give me some getaway time before the two conspirators would realize what I'd done. Joint ownership had put a stake in that idea. I needed an option and with the state my mind was in that afternoon I knew it wasn't going to come to me then.

My last notation about whom I should trust was a reminder to me to be very careful about the people I talked to and what I talked about. I wanted to do nothing that would tip off Sandra or Randall about my knowledge. I pretty much ruled out telling the kids. I was sure one or both of them would spill the beans so they were going to have to be kept in the dark at least as long as their mother.

I did my damndest to act normally that afternoon. As usual on a Sunday evening, it was just Sandra, Merry and me for dinner. Jon was living on campus and we seldom saw him, apart from holidays or when he needed money. I managed to get my emotions under control by the time I picked up the package from the Chinese restaurant. I didn't have much of an appetite but I was determined not to draw attention to myself.

I wasn't very effective at work over the next week. I was constantly trying to work through the problems facing me, coming to terms with the deceit and treachery of my wife. I was going through various stages of emotions: anger, frustration and depression before returning to anger. As for Randall Teller, I was committed to revenge. One way or another he would pay for his sins.

Within a few days, the genesis of one or two ideas began to form. If there were two main objectives for me they were to protect my twenty-fifth anniversary stock award and to somehow extract at least half the equity from our home, if not more. If I focused on just one or two things I would probably be better off.

Gradually, I began to become immune to my feelings when it came to Sandra. If she wanted sex, I gave her every excuse I could think of to avoid it. When I thought she might become suspicious, I reluctantly gave in with none of the enthusiasm I might have previously shown. She didn't seem to notice and on top of that she was much less aggressive herself.

I suspected that was the result of her affair but I monitored her e-mails to Randall just to make sure I hadn't aroused her suspicion. Aside from a reduced sex life, I thought I behaved pretty much as I would have in the past. It wasn't always easy. There were times when I was very angry and had to leave the room to cool off, but I was careful not to portray the rage inside me too obviously.

In every plan there are risks. It was time for me to take the first risk. I phoned my boss, Tom Yardley, and requested an appointment.

At precisely three-thirty on Friday afternoon I presented myself to Tom's secretary and was told to go right in.

"Hi, Dex. Come right in a make yourself comfortable. Would you like a coffee?" he asked, pointing to the carafe on the sideboard.

"Yeah … thanks, Tom." I poured myself a black coffee, my hands not being quite as steady as I would have liked them to be.

"What can I do for you?" he asked.

"Uhhm, Tom … I'd like to talk to you about something very personal and I need to know that what I tell you won't go outside this office."

He gave me the strangest look and was clearly wondering what in the hell this was all about.

"As long as it isn't illegal, Dex, sure. It won't go anywhere from here."

"Thank you. It's a very delicate topic and you'll understand my problem when I lay it out for you."

"Go ahead," he nodded, his eyes riveted on me.

"I have discovered that Sandra is having an affair."

I didn't miss the look of complete astonishment on Tom's face. He knew us very well and I'm sure he was as shocked as I had been with my discovery.

"Are you sure?" he asked, still displaying disbelief.

I handed him a copy of an e-mail I had brought with me. I had blanked out Randall's name just in case he might know him. The e-mail detailed their plot to extract the most money from me they could along with the usual love-talk. I sat quietly as Tom read the message.

"I can't believe it!" he said, shaking his head. "I would never in a million years have thought her capable of something like this."

"Neither did I. Unfortunately, I have about thirty e-mails dating back over a year that indicate how their plan was formed and when they intended to enact it."

"How does this affect Pinecone?" he asked.

"They don't plan to trigger the divorce until I receive the twenty-five hundred shares on my anniversary date. They'll get at least half of that in the divorce and the longer they keep it the more they will be rewarded."

"Jesus Christ, Dex! This is the nastiest thing I've ever heard of. I still can't believe Sandra would agree to take part in it."

"Believe it, Tom. I'm pretty sure her lover is pulling the strings here. He's very knowledgeable about stocks and maybe he's thinking that if he can get the lion's share of my holdings, he can skip with it ... maybe even leaving Sandra holding the bag."

He continued to shake his head in amazement as we talked. Finally, he let out a long sigh and leaned back in his big chair.

"What can I do to help?"

"I need to protect those stocks from falling into the wrong hands. I want you to hold them back until I've rid myself of those two vultures. As long as they are not legally in my possession they can't be claimed as community property in the divorce."

"All right. No problem. What else?"

"Is there any paper around that says you will present me with those stocks on the date of the twenty-fifth anniversary?"

"No. You know me, Tom. Our word has always been good. We work on a handshake and good-faith basis. After nearly twenty-five years, I thought that we knew each other well enough to trust each other."

"Absolutely. I just don't want them claiming that I was entitled to the stock and the paper trail proves it. Right now, as far as they are concerned, it's just hearsay. But that does bring up another point."

He looked at me, waiting for me to continue.

"There's a rumour going around that we might be taken over by a bigger firm. If it's true, will my anniversary award be protected?"

Tom chuckled, shaking his head. "I heard about that rumour and I can assure you it isn't true. Quite the opposite but that's not something I can discuss right now. Rest assured, your job and your anniversary bonus is safe."

"That's good to know, Tom."

"Anything else?"

"Yes … this is a biggee, Tom. I'd like a leave of absence beginning when I've got all my ducks in a row and until my divorce is final or the situation is resolved. However, as far as the outside world is concerned, I'll have resigned and left town and you have no idea when or if I might be back."

"That *is* a biggee, Dex. You run that department. I can promote Dorothy to replace you but that leaves a big hole in our design staff and a problem for me to handle with Dorothy if and when you come back."

"I've thought of that. Are you still looking for a site representative for the Sint Maarten airport job?"

"Yes. Are you volunteering?"

"Yeah. But here's what I want you to do. I don't want you to pay me. It will tip people off that I'm not really gone and the next thing you know word will get out and my wages might be garnisheed. Just set aside what you would pay me and I'll collect it when I'm ready to get the stocks."

"Okay … I guess we can do that. Anything else?"

"Tom … it's got to look like I'm gone for good. We've got a bunch of jobs on the drawing board and there's no reason that I can't be your site guy for some of the less demanding ones. I have some cash and, if I have to, I can live off my RRSP for some time so I won't need immediate access to my salary. I can do my taxes on line so there won't be any trouble that way. All I have to do is set up a mail drop and I should be able to make this work."

"What about the house? You can't just give it to her. Not now."

"No. That one I haven't figured out. The mortgage and the house are in both our names. If I could find a way to have the house in just my name I could mortgage the place to the hilt, pocket the money and leave her stuck with the payments. That part I haven't worked out yet."

"Yeah … that is a problem. It's almost like you have to start all over again," he said, scratching his chin.

"What do you mean?"

"Well, if you put your house up for sale and bought a new one you could probably work it so that the house was just in your name but the mortgage was in both names. That would leave you free to put a second mortgage on the new house. The court would probably order you to make some kind of payments on the mortgage but if you weren't around, well … that would make it her problem, wouldn't it?"

"I'll have to think about that. It sounds complicated but right now I'm damned if I'm going to let them get the equity in that house and leave me with nothing. I worked to get that mortgage down and I want to take advantage of it. I'm sure the courts will ignore that but I'm going to do what I have to do to keep everything I can get my hands on."

"Okay, Dex. Just try and keep everything legal. You want to protect your passport and your future here at Pinecone. I'll do everything I can to support you."

"Thank you, Tom. I really appreciate that. I'll keep you informed of what I plan and let you know my timing. Thanks again," I said as I rose.

Tom got out of his chair and walked with me to the door.

"I'm very sorry about what's happened, Tom. I don't know what to say besides that. I'm still having a hard time thinking Sandra would do this to you ... but ... well, good luck," he said sadly, patting me on the shoulder.

I felt better after talking to Tom. He was one of the originating partners of Pinecone and we had a great relationship. In time he would have to tell Wolf Balak, the other partner, what was going on. Wolf was more involved in the marketing side of the business. He looked for any new opportunity that he thought we could handle and would go after it aggressively. He called on architects and general contractors, keeping our name prominent in their thoughts. He spoke several languages and was invaluable in maintaining the office activity at a high level.

So aside from the home equity, I at least had some kind of plan to deprive my wife and her lover of some of their ill-gotten gains. I was weary after the meeting with Tom so I headed home, not looking forward to the weekend. I was getting tired already of the pretending that everything was normal. That was a bad sign. I had a long way to go before I could trigger my plan and I still had one big hurdle to overcome.

I thought about what Tom had said about buying a new house. When I gave it more of my consideration, I wondered if there wasn't a chance to pull it off. It would take some salesmanship and some trickery but I wasn't above doing anything to salvage something from our home.

"Sandra, I've been thinking," I began one evening later the next week. "With Jon in college and Merry at technical school, I was thinking that maybe we didn't need as big a house any more. We've been in this one for almost twelve years and maybe it's time we found something new just to please ourselves. One of these days in the near future, we're going to be on our own," I finished, waiting to see how she would react.

"What brought this about, Dexter?"

"I don't know. Maybe it's time we looked after ourselves. You know, be a little selfish," I said, wondering how she would react to that comment.

"Do you have somewhere in mind?" she asked, becoming interested.

"That new subdivision up on top of Albion looks interesting. Decent sized lots, quiet neighbourhood, modern houses with all the features and a price we can afford."

"So … you've been thinking about this for a while?" she asked, still a bit surprised.

"Yeah. I mean, wouldn't you like a nice new house with all the latest in appliances and features?"

"I don't know. I haven't thought about it."

"Well, it doesn't cost anything to look. We can go and visit a couple of the show homes and see what you think," I said, hoping she would agree.

"Yes … I guess we could do that," she said, agreeing hesitantly.

"Look … if it's a bad idea just say so. I'm not trying to get you to do something you don't want to do. It's just a suggestion." It was a risky thing to say but I needed to have her agree on her own and not with me pushing her into it.

"No … no. You just took me by surprise. I wasn't expecting this. Come to think of it, I would like to see what a new house has that we don't," she said, sounding a bit more receptive to the idea.

"Well, the show homes will be open on Saturday and Sunday. Why don't we go Saturday afternoon?"

"Sure. Let's do that," she smiled. She sounded more enthusiastic with her answer. Step one of my mission was complete.

We toured the four show homes on Saturday and I very carefully refrained from any negative or overly-positive comments. Some of the decorating was bizarre but I let Sandra decide that for herself. Nevertheless, she had plenty to say about the features and the new things she saw in both layout and decoration. When we left just before they closed up for the day I was pretty sure Sandra was hooked.

"So what did you think about the houses?" I asked as I poured her a glass of wine.

"I liked them. They are so much more modern than this house. I was surprised that the prices weren't as much as I expected they would be."

"Did you see a floor plan you liked?"

"I thought the second house we looked at made the most sense for us," she said, picking up the glossy booklet the agent had given her.

"Well, if you like we could talk to the agent tomorrow and get some specifics about what's included and what's optional."

"Yes … let's do that," she agreed.

I got the impression she was already visualizing moving into a new home. I suspected, however, that she saw Randall in the master bedroom rather than me. Well … we'll see about that.

The floor plan she chose was eighty thousand dollars below the market value of our current house. Even with taxes and fees, it would allow us to make a number of upgrades that would add value to the new home.

"I think we should go for the granite countertops, the Brazilian cherry hardwood floors and the slate tile in the bathrooms and kitchen area. Do you agree?" I asked.

"Yes, as long as we can afford it," she replied.

"By my reckoning, we'll end up with about the same mortgage balance as we have now. It's not as big as our current house but it has all the features we want."

"That would be great, Dexter. I don't look forward to moving but this will be exciting. A new house with everything we want included."

I met with the sales agent on the following Monday afternoon to finalize the sale. I made sure it was in my name alone. He didn't question my request. Perhaps, it wasn't that unusual. It would be seven or eight weeks before the home we chose would be ready for occupancy. It was framed, sheathed and roofed, and the plumbing, electrical and heating were already installed. They were just starting on the insulation.

The next day, I made arrangements to close the existing mortgage and write a new one for the outstanding balance. Sandra's name would be on this document along with mine. I arranged for her to meet me at the bank and we closed off the old mortgage and signed for the new one.

Sandra had contacted a real estate agent she knew and the woman had listed our home at $625k, a little more than I expected. It would leave us some room for negotiation if necessary. I was breathing a little easier at that point. So far, my plan was working.

I dropped into a local branch of an international mortgage broker and met with a gentleman about obtaining a second mortgage. It was supposedly for a vacation property we had our eye on. Naturally, the new house would be put up as collateral and, since the title was in my name, I had no problem in obtaining a commitment for a second mortgage. The amount requested would be $350k, depending upon an assessment the broker would have made on the new property. They were well aware of the first mortgage, and would hold issuance of the additional mortgage until the house was finished and landscaped.

By the time the new home was finished and turned over to us, it was mid-summer. I was becoming very anxious that my escape plan would somehow be discovered but, by monitoring the e-mails between Sandra and Randall, I couldn't see any evidence that either of them was suspicious.

In fact, Sandra was praising me for suggesting the new home and delighted with all the features it had. Mr. Teller was downplaying the whole thing, his emails suggesting that not long from now they would be together and that new home would be theirs. I couldn't figure out how Randall thought he would be able to dump his wife and move in with mine and not have a big financial burden to carry in supporting two families.

My getaway was inching closer now. As soon as the appraisal was done, I would obtain the second mortgage and put my final plan into place. Those funds would be deposited into my business account. I met with a different financial investment company where I was assured that I could transfer my RRSP account to any of their branches anywhere in the world. They also assured me that my agent could not block any move that I wished to make, even though it was to another company. That was a relief.

"I'm getting close to being ready to go, Tom," I told my boss.

"Have you got everything you need?" he asked. I could see the unhappiness on his face.

"Yes. Your suggestion about a new mortgage was the answer and I've got all the pieces in place now. I've made another decision, though. I don't plan to divorce Sandra."

He looked surprised. "Oh ... have you had a change of heart?"

"No ... not at all. I just don't want to bother with lawyers and courts and the possibility of alimony that I would never intend to pay. I'm just going to disappear. You, of course, will be one of the very few people who know where I am so I'm counting on you to keep the dogs at bay."

"How will I know where you are? You quit, didn't you? You don't work here any more, do you? I won't have any idea of what to tell anyone who asks me about you, especially Sandra," he grinned.

It was the first time I'd seen anything resembling a smile out of Tom in some time. I hated to go but we both knew it was necessary and we both knew that he wouldn't really be losing me. We arranged a business meeting with dinner on the eve of my departure at a very nice restaurant that neither of us had been to before. Little chance of our being recognized, we thought.

And so it was done. My life in Maple Ridge was coming to a close. Whether it was temporary or not remained to be seen. My twenty-three year marriage to Sandra was also coming to a close. She didn't know it of course. I was supposedly going on a weeklong road trip to review some new software programs, starting on a Sunday night. I already knew she planned to get together with Randall the moment I was out the door.

I was scheduled out on a late Sunday afternoon KLM flight to Amsterdam, overnight at the Radisson, on to Paris by train Monday, then Air France to St. Martin on Friday. It was the long way around, but it would throw anyone trying to follow me off the track for a while. Besides, a few days in Paris would be good for my spirits. In many ways, I was going into exile ... voluntarily to be sure, but all the same it was exile.

Almost everything I did to arrange my escape was done on my laptop computer. The plane and hotel reservations, the transfer of funds from my business account to a new international bank, the cashing in of my whole life policies and ultimately, the transfer of my RRSP out of the grasp of Randall Teller and into another safe haven.

It took until Thursday evening before Sandra realized she hadn't heard from me. Perhaps sooner, but that was when I saw the e-mail from her.

Where are you, Dexter? You haven't called. Are you all right? Why aren't you answering your cell phone? Please call me, I'm worried.
Love, Sandra.

She had sent it at eleven that morning, probably just before she got ready to go to work at one that afternoon. Normally, she would have heard from me no later than Monday, then Wednesday before I came home on Friday. That was my routine for the last few years when I was travelling. This was different. I assumed by Friday or at the latest Monday, she would be on the phone to Tom asking about my whereabouts.

Randall would be alerted to the move of the RRSP the day I left Paris for St. Martin. That, combined with my "failure to communicate" would let him and Sandra know that I was onto them. That same Friday, Tom would mail a package containing copies of all the e-mails to Mrs. Teller. With all these things happening in a matter of a couple of days, life was going to be very chaotic for the two lovebirds.

I had arranged for the second mortgage to be automatically paid from my new account. With any luck, they'd be a long time figuring out that I owned the house and the new mortgage. The longer it took for them to realize just how much I had screwed them out of, the better I'd feel about it. On top of that, they would have to give up hope of getting their hands on the Pinecone stock. After all, if I had quit I couldn't claim the twenty-five-year bonus, could I? It was one of the few things that gave me pleasure in a time when there was precious little pleasure in my life.

Sandra was sending a continuous stream of e-mails that I was deleting, most of them without reading. I wasn't going to respond to any e-mails other than from Tom Yardley. I wasn't sure when he'd tell Wolf Balak about my situation but I'd let him decide that. At some point, I knew I'd hear from my son and daughter but again, I wasn't going to respond for another week or so. I didn't want to torture them but I also didn't want to reveal what was going on. I would leave it to their mother to tell them what was happening. I would definitely be interested to hear her version. My parents didn't use the internet so they had no way of communicating with me, nor I with them. I would have to deal with that in due time.

There was only one plan of revenge for Mr. Randall Teller. It would be the fallout from sending his wife copies of the e-mails between her husband and Sandra. Without a return address, it would appear that the package came from a local address. I had to be satisfied that my actions would produce a shit-storm of grief for one Mr. Randall Teller.

Chapter 3
Sunshine and Lollipops

For the first two weeks in the Caribbean I was in paradise. Brilliant, hot sun, azure blue sea, cheap booze and fresh seafood. I acquired a straw hat, a pair of sandals and some Bermuda shorts that passed for dress wear on this island.

It took me a couple of days to find a place to live. I had been advised that Sint Maarten was the cheaper place to reside. It made sense to live there anyway, since the airport and our construction site was on that side. I found a small, three-room flat above a trinket shop in Philipsburg and settled in. I didn't need much. I ate out every day and used the place only to sleep and occasionally to write my reports to Tom Yardley.

Fortunately, the island had a high-speed wireless internet provider so document and drawing transfer weren't a problem. I had a portable office on the site that contained a computer, a printer and a plotter. It also had an air conditioner, essential in what was otherwise a tin box.

My job was to liaise with the construction crew at the airport. They were American so no language problem was expected. They were quite competent but some of their day workers were less than efficient. As a result, the job would take longer than I was accustomed to. I hated to think how long it would be if it were a local contractor.

The temporary agent we employed had been on the job two months and had overseen the site location and footings before I arrived. We spent a half day discussing what was going on and what I should be on the look-out for. Shortcuts were common in this part of the world, especially if there was money to be gained from them.

I had been on the island a little more than a week when I made contact with my son, Jon. He was living in Antofagasta, Chile, working almost eight thousand feet up in the Andes at a copper mine. He was only at his home on the weekends but we both had Skype and luckily the connection was good.

"Hi Jon, how are you?"

"Good Dad, but you've sure got everyone upset with you disappearing like you did."

"Yeah ... I'm sure I have. What did your mother say about my reason for leaving?"

"Nothing. She said she couldn't imagine why you'd run off like that. She sounds pretty upset, Dad. Why did you go?"

"I'm disappointed that she couldn't bring herself to tell you the truth, Jon. She was having an affair with our financial advisor and planned to divorce me and take everything she could with her. I'll send you a couple of her e-mails to lover-boy and you'll get the drift pretty quick."

"Why, Dad? What would make her want to do something like that? I don't understand it."

"Neither do I, Jon. She's not at the stage where she's ready to face what she did so I guess we'll just wait until she can confess her deeds."

"Where are you, Dad? Are you still in Vancouver?"

"No ... I'm out of the country. If you promise not to tell anyone, I'm in the Caribbean. I have a job and I intend to stay here for some time. Please don't tell your mother or sister. I don't want to deal with your mother just now. I'm sure she hasn't told Merry what she did.

Merry's pretty upset with me by the sound of her e-mails. I just quit responding to them. Have you heard from her?"

"Yeah, sure. Several times. You're right; she's pretty pissed with you. Figures you've run off with some floozy and left them high and dry. I think she ought to know the truth, Dad."

"Let's leave it for a while and see if your mother can come to terms with what she's done. I've sent the e-mails she was exchanging with her boyfriend to his wife. The guy's got five kids, for Christ sakes. Can you image what will happen when the courts get ahold of him?"

"Maybe that's why Mom's not working at that office any more. I don't know if she quit or got, but she's looking for another job."

"Interesting. Sounds like things are getting a little hairy for her," I chuckled.

"Dad ... is this the way it's going to be ... I mean ... you hating Mom? I know she did something very wrong but ... Merry and I ... we have to stay in touch with her. We can't just abandon her. It wouldn't be right even if she did what you said."

"Yeah ... I guess I understand that. If you're talking to your sister have her call me on Skype, preferably when her mother isn't around. I'd like to talk to her and explain."

"Sure, Dad, I can do that. Are we in the same time zone? It's just past eleven o'clock here."

"We're an hour behind you. It's four hours difference to Vancouver from here."

"Okay. I'll try and set something up with Merry and get her to call on the weekends like you do."

"Thanks, Jon. Good to talk to you. I wish it was about something a little brighter but I'm afraid I don't see that happening for some time."

"Take care, Dad. Bye."

Well, at least we had a conversation that didn't end in recriminations over my actions. I think maybe Jon understood why I took off and I could understand why he would want to stay in touch with his mother. What a mess! Now I would have to explain myself to Merry. I wasn't looking forward to that.

I e-mailed Jon four messages from Sandra's file that pretty well told the story of their plan. I found four that weren't too sexually explicit. I didn't think that kind would help smooth the waters for anyone.

It didn't take me long to find a routine for my day-to-day work. It wasn't very demanding to be honest. I wandered about the site introducing myself to the various contractors and vendors as the opportunity arose. It was when I met the two people representing the prime lenders on this project that things got interesting. They were women, twins in fact, and they were quite a sight.

They were in their mid thirties, I guessed. They were clearly identical twins and two more formidable women I had yet to meet. They were definitely sun worshipers if their bleach-blonde hair and tanned bodies were any indication. They were also physically fit despite their size. If I were to guess, they would be at least five-ten and possibly one-hundred-and-eighty pounds. But from what I could see they were not fat … just big.

"Good afternoon, ladies," I announced politely. "I am Dexter McLeod and I represent Pinecone Engineering. We are responsible for the design and plans for this project."

"Hallo, Mister McLeod, nice to meet you," one of them said. "I am Adriaana de Groot and this is my sister, Katerina. We are with ABN Amro. We are financing this project for the government of Sint Maarten. We are here to see that our monies are correctly used."

She had a big voice to go with her big body but the tone of her voice and her infectious smile weren't intimidating at all. Her English was very good, tinged as it was with a Dutch accent.

"Well then," I said, "we should be seeing a great deal of each other over the next few months. I am here to see that this addition is built according to the plans. Like you, I'm here to protect the investors' dollars ... or should I say guilders."

"Euros, Mr. McLeod," Katerina said quietly but with a similar smile and tone as her sister. "We can work well together I think."

We had got off on the right foot and I was pleased with that. I liked their outlook and yet I could hear the no-nonsense attitude toward their responsibilities. I wondered how they had come to be chosen for this job and why both of them?

"Have you done this type of work before?" I asked.

"Yes, this is our third project. Our company has investments in Aruba that we needed to ... secure. Also, almost two years in Curacao building a bridge."

"Well, sounds like you've really gotten to see a good part of the Caribbean and gained a lot of experience," I said.

"Yes ... it has been very interesting but I think soon it is time to go home," Adriaana said.

"Where do you call home?"

"Utrecht. It is in the south from Amsterdam," she replied.

I was getting the impression that she was the spokesperson for the two. Katerina seemed to be a little quieter ... more reserved. No matter, they were quite an impressive pair and I was pleased that we seemed to hit it off quite well.

"And where is your home?" Adriaana asked.

"Vancouver ... in Canada," I said, not wishing to complicate my answer.

"Oh ... yes ... of course. We have many relatives living near Vancouver. Do you know the town, Pitt Meadows?"

"Yes ... of course. It is right next door to where I live ... I mean ... used to live."

"There are many Dutch people living in your town?" Katerina asked quietly.

"Yes indeed, quite a few. They came after the Second World War and settled there. They taught us how to dike and reclaim the land that would flood each year. They have made good citizens," I said emphatically.

"I am certain we have relatives living there now," Adriaana said with some confidence.

"I wouldn't be surprised. De Groot is a common name. They might be greenhouse growers or dairy farmers."

"Oh, we have so much to talk about," Adriaana enthused. "We must sometime have a nice conversation."

"I'd like that. You ladies name the time and I'll try and be there."

As I walked back to the engineering portable, I found it interesting that the two women would work as a pair. On top of that, they were on the site every day from what I could see. That was unusual for a financial overseer. I expected they would spend their time examining purchase orders, invoices and estimates. You didn't often see them in the field, close to the action.

The two ladies arrived and left in an ancient hot pink Citroen 2CV, the iconic post-war French mini car. While it looked ridiculous to many eyes, it had been in production for decades, so it must have some redeeming features. Around here cars were a luxury with expensive gasoline, limited roads and the hopelessness of getting repairs. As a result, older cars were the norm for many of the residents.

Merry called me on Skype just before noon on Saturday. She had obviously been talking to Jon because her tone of voice was a lot more civil than her previous e-mails.

"Hello, Daddy. How are you? I miss you?" she said sadly.

"I know. I miss you too, Sweetheart. I'm sorry things have turned out the way they have. Has your mother told you why I left?"

"Yes. When Jon told me about the e-mails you sent him, I confronted her and she finally confessed. She's very ashamed of what she did … especially since it was all for nothing."

"Jon said she wasn't working at Teller's office any more. Is that true?"

"Yes. There was some kind of problem. Auditors came in and were going through his records. They questioned Mom several times over a few days before they said she was okay. They never did say what it was about but Mom thinks there maybe something wrong with some of the accounts. Then she heard his wife was divorcing him. I guess I should have been more suspicious about them. I just couldn't believe Mom would do something like that."

"Yeah. I know what you mean, Merry. I'm still wondering why. What did I do … or not do … that caused this?"

"She's not opening up very much, Dad, but I got her to admit she knew why you left and who was involved. I don't know much more than that."

"Well, that's enough for now. As long as you know the truth, I'm okay with it."

"When are you coming home, Dad? When am I going to see you again?"

"I've got a job and I can't get away until it's finished. I'm not in Canada as you've probably guessed. I promise we'll keep in touch just like today. Are you all right for money, dear?"

"Yes. I have a job waiting for me when I graduate next month. I'm going to work with one of the big developers in town. I'm really excited about it. I'll just be an apprentice for a while but it sounds like a great opportunity and I'm really pleased I'm getting the chance."

"That's great, Merry. I'm very proud of you. Congratulations. I want to hear all about it when you get settled."

"I promise. Bye Daddy. I love you."

I sat back in my chair, a few tears at the ready. I was happy that Merry and I had reconciled over the actions of her mother. It would have been very hurtful if she had gone on being angry and disappointed in me. The fact that she had to force the truth out of her mother didn't do anything to lessen my anger at Sandra. If I hadn't shed many tears it was because I was so angry at her deceit. I'd lost a lot of sleep in the last month or more thinking about what she'd done.

Nevertheless, I missed the good parts of our marriage. Not just the sex, but the companionship and closeness that we had shared. For almost all of our twenty-three years I had felt an attachment beyond just the formalities of marriage. It was an emotional bond and when that was broken, so too was I. Some things can't be fixed when they are damaged and our marriage was one of them.

I purchased a used Vespa scooter from a local garage. It had originally been bought in Germany and brought to the island ten years ago. I had no idea what year it was, but it ran, started without too much fuss and smoked only a little. It sipped gasoline and that was important with the cost being what it was here.

I developed a routine quite quickly. I would meet with the prime contractor's manager each morning to discuss any issues that might come up. I was not an engineer, but over the two decades I had spent designing various structures, I could converse intelligently with them and forward any issues to the office for review via e-mail. I was not expected to revise designs on the spot.

I saw the twins often over the next two months and I had taken to calling them the "dynamic duo," a compliment in my mind. We had begun socializing on occasion, stopping at one of the local cafés for a coffee and a pastry.

"Do they always call you Dexter?" Adriaana asked one morning.

"No, my friends call me Dex," I replied.

"I am Adi to my friends, and of course my sister is Kat. You may call us by those names," she smiled.

"Thank you, and feel free to call me Dex. So … we've become Adi, Kat, and Dex then."

"Wonderful!" Adi said, clapping her hands together. "We must have dinner together this weekend. Please say you will."

"I'd like that. Where would you like to go?"

"Oh, no. You do not understand. You would be our guest at our home. We insist. Kat is a very good cook."

"How can I refuse then," I grinned, looking at Kat and seeing her pleasure at my acceptance.

Friday evening, I rode my little Vespa up the hill on the northeast side of Phillipsburg, following the directions the twins had given me. They lived in a very nice flat-roofed, one-level house off Guana Bay Road, with a wonderful view out to the east and south. I wondered how they could afford to stay here.

"Hello, ladies, here I am," I announced myself as I knocked on the already open front door.

"Come in, Dex," I heard from the back of the house.

As I entered, I immediately smelled something wonderful wafting though the large living area. I simply followed that aroma and quickly found a big, fully tiled kitchen with the two ladies bustling about, preparing the meal.

"My, my. Whatever it is smells terrific," I enthused.

"Thank you," Kat said somewhat shyly. She definitely had a different personality from her sister.

All the windows and doors were open, so I assumed there was no air conditioning in the house. Nonetheless, a slightly cooling breeze was evident as the sun had begun to set and the breeze off the sea had picked up. It would be almost nine before we ate but that was traditional in this climate.

Both women were dressed in loose fitting full body gowns, not unlike a Muumuu in Hawaii. Adi's was decorated in a variety of leaf patterns, varying from pastel, to leaf, to forest green in colour. It was very attractive. Kat's was a seashell pattern in blues, purples, and greys. It took me a minute to realize the ladies weren't wearing brassieres as the sway of their full breasts moved freely under the light fabric.

"Cold beer is in the cooler, Dex. Please take one," Adi said.

"Thank you, I will," I replied, opening the little refrigerator door and taking out a Heineken. The twins already had drinks on the counter but were busy with the meal at present. As I watched them I wondered if they knew just how enticing they were. Perhaps it was just me and my self-imposed hiatus from women, but they appealed to me in a very visceral way.

Adi finished up what she was doing and joined me at the entrance to the kitchen.

"You have a lovely home here, Adi. Is it yours?"

"No … it is rented by our company for this project. We don't know who owns it but they are not from this island. We think they are from Holland. We are very happy to have it. It is very nice and quite big for the two of us. Would you like to see it?"

"Yes, please."

She took me through a portal to the rear of the house. There was an area I would call a laundry and mudroom, with a door to the back yard. A bedroom with a double bed, a large bathroom, all tiled like the kitchen and another room that looked like it had been set up as an office.

I looked out the window into the back yard and saw nothing but shrubs and trees. It didn't look like there was a yard but I did see a concrete patio area with a large, rectangular umbrella. Altogether it was a very nice home for the ladies.

The master suite was large and dominating it was a very big king-size bed. There were a couple of wardrobe cupboards, two dressers and two night tables. I took it from that that both women slept in the same bed. I was about to say something but thought better of it. A small but complete ensuite bathroom was included as well. As I looked back at the bed before leaving, I thought what a great playground that would make.

"This looks like a very nice place to live," I remarked.

"Yes," Adi agreed. "A big room for guests, but we have not yet taken a chance to do that. Perhaps we will have visitors in the winter season."

She took my empty beer bottle and quickly replaced it with a fresh one. I thanked her and again admired just how attractive she and her sister were. I think she might have noticed my gaze but said nothing, turning back to the kitchen to help Kat.

I wondered how I would tell them apart when they weren't speaking. It was the only discernable difference between them. I had been around them long enough to recognize a slight difference in their speech and certainly in their tone of voice. Adi was the established leader and Kat was the quiet, reserved follower. It occurred to me that they might be lesbians but if they were, they didn't give off any hints to that possibility. I preferred to believe they were straight. It suited my growing fantasies much better.

The twins represented a total opposite from Sandra in sexual attraction. Their deeply tanned and toned bodies, despite their size, were becoming an obsession with me. I found myself staring at them when I thought they wouldn't notice. Like that works, right!

"Dex, you are looking at us with hungry eyes. Perhaps it is time to eat, yes?" Adi said slyly.

Busted! Caught red-handed while I daydreamed.

"Uhhm ... yeah ... sure ... sorry," was about all I could manage as I scrambled to hide my embarrassment.

"You should not apologize. Women want to know they are attractive to a man. It makes us feel very ... warm."

That didn't help. I was a complete amateur at flirting and I was up against an expert in Adi. I glanced at Kat and saw her trying to hide her giggles behind her hand. She wasn't very good at it. I wasn't sure where this was going but as long as they didn't throw me out I would try and make something out of this little game.

"I have a question that's been bothering me," I said. "How can I tell you two apart ... I mean visually? I know there's a difference when you speak but I can't *see* any difference. So until one of you says something, I'm never sure who I'm talking to."

Adi laughed heartily turning to her twin. Kat's laughter was more of a tinkling, little-girl sound. Adi turned back to me, unbuttoning the top two buttons on her smock and pulling back the left side. Just above her left breast was a modest tattoo of the letter A in a stylish script. She turned to Kat.

Kat seemed a bit shy but followed Adi's lead and showed me her tattoo, the letter K in the same script.

"Now you know how to tell who you are with," Adi said with delight. She was having fun teasing me and to be honest, I didn't mind a bit.

"Well, ladies, unless you go around in some very revealing tops or very small bikinis, not many people are going to see those initials."

"Which do you prefer?" Adi asked with a raised eyebrow. "Or perhaps you would like to be surprised."

"I'll have to give that some thought," I said, ducking the question and hoping the meal would be served soon.

Katerina saved the day. "It is time to eat. We can talk about tattoos later if you like." Even she was getting in on the teasing.

Adi was right, Kat was a very fine cook and the fish dish was something I hadn't experienced before. Beautifully prepared and served, I really enjoyed the meal and of course, the company. The light banter had kept up but without the teasing that had preceded it.

"This fish is wonderful, Kat. What is it?"

"Tilefish," she smiled, pleased with the compliment. "It is one of the most popular, like grouper and swordfish. When I go to market I never know what they will have. Today it was this."

"I like it. Very nice. Thank you," I smiled sincerely. She had served it on a bed of coarse, brown rice, with a light salad on the side. It really was excellent.

I helped the ladies with what few dishes needed to be washed. With the three of us in the kitchen, body contact was inevitable. Adi made sure to rub me several times as she went by, using her breasts and butt to make contact. She was about as subtle as a sledgehammer. I kept my eye on Kat who was trying to suppress her giggles as Adi shamelessly taunted me.

As this little game continued, I decided to participate and at the first opportunity I lightly slapped Adi's butt as she passed by.

"Oh my goodness that was naughty, Mr. McLeod," she said, once again displaying the raised eyebrow.

"You, young lady, are a tease," I replied. "You are tempting me to misbehave, Ms. de Groot."

"Am I so? Tell me about this misbehaviour," she said as she stepped toward me.

"You are tempting me to lay my hands on your lovely body. It would be quite rude of me to do that when you have been such kind hostesses."

"And just where would those hands be on this lovely body," she smirked, now only inches from me.

"I'm not sure there is any place that would be safe."

"Oh, am I in danger?" she asked. "Will you help me, Kat?" she said, never taking her eyes off me.

I hadn't noticed Kat standing just to my side, watching this little play between Adi and myself. A quick look told me she was fascinated by what was happening. Was this something new for her or both of them? Only one way to find out.

"Please excuse my forwardness but I believe I should personally thank you both for your hospitality this evening," I said as I reached for Adi and pulled her to me. I looked into her eyes and then slowly closed the gap, kissing her firmly on the lips.

When we broke, I could see the surprise in Adi's eyes and wondered if I'd gone too far. My unspoken question was quickly answered when she pulled me to her and pressed her mouth on mine, her tongue probing as she did. My hands dropped to her lovely, big ass cheeks and began to stroke them. After a few moments we broke the kiss.

"I think I should properly thank the cook, don't you?" I grinned.

I moved to Kat and took her in my arms. She willing submitted to my kiss but didn't offer any tongue. She wasn't uncomfortable but wasn't as aggressive as her sister. My suspicions about her were correct. She was a bit shy but not painfully so.

"You are very kind with your praise, Dex," Kat said, now showing a slight smile.

"I meant every word of it."

This little play had gone a great deal further than I expected and now I wasn't sure where it would go from here. I know what I wanted to have happen but I could ruin everything if I presumed too much and Adi called a halt to the game. Best to let her and Kat decide what next.

They both moved in on me and the next thing I knew the two of them were holding me captive in their embrace. I placed my arms around their shoulders and the three of us were immobile in the centre of the kitchen. I leaned to Kat first, kissing her lightly then moving to Adi and repeating the gesture.

I knew things were going to progress from there when I felt and hand slide down the front of my shorts and trace the outline of my rising erection. The three of us were busy kissing and nibbling as we stood there. I squeezed a butt cheek on each of them and got a squeeze from Adi on my cock. There wasn't much doubt any more about where this was going to end up.

Adi undid the belt on my shorts, opened them and let them drop to my ankles. She slipped her hand inside my briefs and grasped my cock, stroking then squeezing it gently. A moment later I felt a second hand softly close over my scrotum, rolling the contents back and forth in her hand. It turned out Kat wasn't shy at all when it came to participating.

Adi stepped back and with a single movement, pulled her gown up over her head and discarded it. She was naked except for a thong covering only the barest essentials of her womanhood and she confirmed my suspicions that she was tanned everywhere. She moved back to me and began unbuttoning my shirt and with Kat's help had me naked except for my briefs. I was so damned hard that I could barely stand it. Both women were running their hands over me and somewhere along the way Kat had lost her gown.

I could feel the big, soft breasts of Kat rubbing my back as her hands once again slipped down into my briefs. Adi was holding my head as she buried her tongue into my mouth while I had both hands on her breasts, my thumbs stroking her nipples to their own prominent erection. I couldn't recall being in a more erotic situation than this. I wasn't going anywhere other than to the bedroom with these gorgeous females.

I had never been involved in a threesome and while I knew about them, I had no idea how to react. My first thought was how could I satisfy both these women? I had a feeling I was going to be called upon to perform beyond anything I had ever attempted and I hoped I wouldn't embarrass myself.

My two beautiful hostesses led me to their pleasure palace and within seconds, all three of us were naked. I could see the two tattoos and could easily tell which of the sisters I was with. But there was another difference. While Adi had a completely shaven mound, Kat had a neatly trimmed small triangle almost pointing to her target. So there was another way to tell them apart.

We spent a lot of time with foreplay which helped me control myself. I hadn't had sex in over two months and even then it wasn't enjoyable. I was faking it with Sandra at the time and there was no pleasure involved. This would be completely different. I had no second thoughts about whether I was doing the right thing.

If there was a surprise that night it was Kat. She may have been the quieter of the two twins but she was sexually hotter than a furnace. I lost track of the number of times I would switch partners and provide either oral sex or slide my cock into one or the other of these wanton women. Every now and then I would look for the tattoo to see which of them I was involved with but, after a while, I really didn't care.

I substituted my mouth and fingers when I was sure I couldn't raise an erection one more time but I received no complaints and in fact one or the other of them would use their mouths, tongues and fingers to try and bring me back to life. How I survived as long as I did was a big surprise to me. Maybe it was because I had been without for a while but more likely it was due to the sexual attention paid to me by these two incredible women.

There was never a question that I would leave and go back to my little apartment. I didn't have the strength anyway. We slept in a tangled mass of bodies and wet sheets, but none of us seemed to care. When I awoke in the morning, I was alone.

As I lay there, I pondered why I didn't feel guilty. I was still married to Sandra so technically this was adultery on my part, just as she had committed with Teller. Yet, I really didn't have any regrets. Odd? I was still angry with my wife but … but what? Was this the beginning of whoever I was to become in the future? Forget the past, live for today … and then tomorrow?

I could hear activity in the kitchen so I rose, pulled on my briefs and shorts and padded toward the sounds.

"Good morning, Dex," Kat said with a big smile. I knew it was her because her tattooed initial was showing along with her magnificent breasts and most of the rest of her body. She was wearing a waist-high apron and little more. As she turned, I could see the thin straps of a thong disappearing into her ass crack. She was no longer the shy one.

"Good morning my lovely ladies," I said. Kat came over to me and wrapped her arms around my neck and gave me a soul-scorching kiss.

"Go and brush your teeth," she said, her finger poking me in the chest.

"Yes, ma'am." I knew when I had been dismissed. I was back in a couple of minutes. I didn't want to miss the show.

"Did you sleep well," Adi asked.

"I must have. I have no memory of when we ended our time together until I woke just a few minutes ago. I hope I didn't disappoint you," I said, fishing for some kind of feedback.

Adi came to me and gave me the same mouth-to-mouth treatment as Kat had earlier.

"You were very good, Dex. Very strong and most satisfying. We will have to do this much more in the future. Kat … do you agree?"

She turned and smiled. "Oh yes, many more times I am hoping."

I breathed a sigh of relief. If they were happy I was delirious. I felt like I'd just been awarded a lifetime membership in the Playboy club with all the benefits and some they didn't offer.

Kat was making pannekoeks, she said. Dutch pancakes. They were very good, sprinkled with fresh lime juice and a bit of sugar. No syrup was needed. With some fresh fruit juice and coffee, it was the perfect start to the day. After breakfast I discovered that my lovely ladies had the day all planned out for us.

Kat handed me a clean white t-shirt with something written in Dutch on it. She had hand-washed my shirt from yesterday, hung it on a line in the laundry area, telling me it would dry by evening. The ladies wore a loose, coarse cotton blouse which at first I though would be too warm for them. However, they had decided to go without their brassieres again and the heavier material would prevent any embarrassment. Their skin-tight shorts and sandals completed their skimpy wardrobe. We were off to spend another fine day on our island in the sun.

Chapter 4
Fool's Paradise?

In the beginning, my relationship with Adi and Kat was confined to the weekends, usually Friday evening, Saturday and returning back to my little place on Sunday noon. During the week each of us was dedicated to our responsibilities and confined our relationship to the occasional morning coffee and conversation if we were in the same vicinity. I have to confess that I was as happy as hell with what had happened. I was involved with two very amazing women, amazons I suppose you could call them. They filled my dreams at night and made them all come true on the weekends.

European women have very liberal ideas about relationships. I had some time to think about where my two ladies and I were headed in the future. Our project would last another fourteen months unless unforeseen problems arose. What then? The more time I spent with Adi and Kat, the more I wanted to spend.

It wasn't just the sex, although that part of our time together was incredible. We were so compatible in other ways. We enjoyed being around each other, whether it was a trip to Marigot for a little French cuisine and shopping or just relaxing on the back patio, getting some sun and talking about anything that came to mind. Strangely, I continued to feel no guilt about being intimate with them despite the fact that I was still married. That was uncharacteristic for the "old me."

It took me a while to tell the ladies about the disastrous end to my marriage. They were suitably shocked when I told them of Sandra's plot but not totally surprised that a woman of her age might take a lover. We had been sitting on the back patio one Saturday evening and, after one more beer than I should have had, I opened up to them.

"Dex," Adi began as I finished my story, "ladies ... as we get older ... we are afraid if we can attract a man. Look at us. To be sure we are not beautiful Paris models. We are the fat girls from school. The boys made fun of us. We had no lovers to catch us. Someday we might marry a farmer or such who was lonely but there would be no prince to come for us.

"Kat had dreams. I had dreams. We wanted a handsome man like you, Dex. But he did not come. We learned we were not beautiful but still we looked for a man who might love us. As we got older it was hard. Not so many men to find for us. Sometimes, a man would tell us nice things about how we looked and we might take him to our bed. We would want to believe him but it was not always the truth.

"Your wife ... Sandra ... perhaps she was afraid that she was not so pretty to the men. If a man like this Randall would tell her of her beauty she could believe it because she wanted it to be so. She was foolish. She did not remember what a good man she had already. She will learn. It will hurt her but ... she will learn."

I sat for a while, digesting Adi's words. Was it as simple as that? Did she get distracted by a man who complimented her on her looks when all along I knew just how beautiful she was? Was it that easy for Randall to seduce her? I hoped not but it *had* happened.

I was remembering a story from my great-grandfather on my father's side. He recalled having an old Model T Ford in the early thirties. Many of the roads where he lived in northern Ontario were still gravel or even dirt and over time and with the effect of rain, deep ruts would form in the roads and the tires would naturally follow whatever direction the ruts went. When it came time to turn off the road, it took a great deal of effort to slowly climb out of the ruts to go in another direction.

My life had been like that, I realized. I had created my own rut. My routine, which satisfied me in so many ways, was the rut. I was predictable. I took Sandra for granted even though I admired her beauty. I must have forgotten to tell her often enough. My family and friends could count on me because I *was* predictable. I offered them little in the way of surprise because I *was* predictable. And then, when Randall came along, he used that against me.

When I discovered Sandra's affair I did something completely unpredictable. I had extracted whatever measure of revenge and salvaged what I could, something no one would have expected. I had disappeared, leaving no hint where I had gone. I had climbed out of the rut and gone off in another direction and in doing so had found these two extraordinary women.

"Adi, Kat, I will not have you talking about yourselves that way. You are beautiful to me. You are not fat and you are not without admirers. I see the way men look at you and I see the way they look at me with envy. I don't have just one lovely woman on my arm, I have two. I think of myself as a very, very, lucky man."

My little speech brought smiles to their faces and we gather each other into our arms and kissed while we hugged. I had a feeling of contentment and satisfaction that I hadn't felt in a long time. But it didn't answer the question. When the project was done, what would become of us?

Whatever we had set in motion that afternoon, it produced a change in our relationship. It didn't take very much convincing on their part when the twins suggested I move in with them. I hesitated at first, wondering if that would produce a problem but they were so persuasive that it was the right thing for the three of us that I put my doubts aside and agreed.

I packed up what little I had from my apartment, loaded it into their Citroen and left for the de Groot residence the next day. There wasn't any question about where I would sleep. I was to be with them in the big bed. I would use the wardrobe in the spare bedroom for my clothes but I would sleep with the ladies. I had no intention of arguing against that.

On Monday morning, I was reminded that these ladies were all business on a business day. They rose at six, did their bathroom duties, made breakfast and sat with their morning coffee, discussing what needed to be done on the job that day. It was interesting to me that they too had their routine. Perhaps we are all creatures of habit.

What followed was fourteen months of blissful existence in my temporary paradise. The project moved steadily forward, although at a painfully slow pace. There were no problems with the engineering drawings or calculations, and I found I wasn't working very hard on behalf of Pinecone. I kept in touch with Tom and he was satisfied with my reports, letting me know he hadn't heard from Sandra or anyone else for quite some time. I felt secure in my exile.

As the time of completion came nearer, I could sense the change in the twins. I suppose they could sense a change in me too. It was on my mind but I still hadn't come to terms with what I would do after this project was finished. It was Adi who broached the subject.

"Dex, what will you do when this work is done? Where will you go?"

"I don't know, Adi. I know I have to decide. I just don't know," I admitted.

"You might come with us," Kat said softly.

"Where?" I asked.

"Holland. We have a nice home. You would be welcome there."

"Perhaps first you need to mend your life in Vancouver, Dex," Adi suggested.

"That's probably what I'll have to do ... sooner or later. I need to deal with my marriage and then maybe I can decide what to do."

Our last two weeks in Sint Maarten was filled with signing off on the completion of the project. The girls would be staying behind for another few days to attend the official opening of the airport addition, since they were the bank's representatives. I met with the general contractor and he thanked me for my cooperation and assistance. My work was done. I had sent Tom an e-mail a couple of weeks earlier that I was coming back to Vancouver to "face the music" as I put it.

In fact, I had decided I needed to formalize the end of my relationship with Sandra. I would file for divorce but I would set the terms. If they were unacceptable I would simply disappear again. I had already proven that it wasn't that hard.

The twins and I had a tearful goodbye at the airport on a Monday afternoon as I boarded a commuter flight to Puerto Rico, then Miami, Chicago and finally, Vancouver. It would be a long journey but with my mind settled, I was almost looking forward to it. Adi and Kat were doing their best to smile but I knew they were thinking they would never see me again.

I was either in the air or sitting in some airport lounge over the next thirty-seven hours and it gave me plenty of time to think. I hadn't used much of my cash. Living costs with the ladies were almost nothing aside from food and drink. Their employers paid for their accommodation. I sold the scooter for almost what I had paid for it and a cheap suitcase looked after the clothes I had purchased. Tom would have set aside whatever my salary was for this job. I had passed my anniversary date two months earlier and I could now think about what I wanted to do with my shares.

I prepared a written list of what I was willing to offer Sandra in the divorce. It was generous in my mind, considering her betrayal. It would be a take-it-or-leave-it offer with no negotiations. I wouldn't be hiring a lawyer until she had agreed to the proposal. Then it would be a matter of formalizing the agreement.

The only cool weather clothes I had taken with me were a breathable shell for rain and a sweatshirt for cool weather. I think I might have worn the sweatshirt three or four times, no more. When I landed in Vancouver it was 5°C (41°F) with a foggy drizzle. Exactly what I expected in late January. I hailed a cab and made for the downtown hotel I had reserved.

It seemed strange as I travelled the familiar, dark, rain-soaked streets of my hometown. Not much appeared to have changed in the last year-and-a-half. There was no point in going out to Maple Ridge. I was sure Sandra would have thrown out all my clothes. I was also sure I would have to meet with her at least once in the next while and I had to wonder what kind of reception I would get. Anger? Sorrow? Regret?

And what about Randall? What had become of him? The package of e-mails I had sent to Mrs. Teller must have precipitated the divorce action Merry told me about. I had extracted my RRSP from Randall's clutches and transferred it to another firm located in downtown Vancouver. Tom had vouched for them as responsible and honest so I left my affairs in their hands. I would need an update from them and I made a note to get an appointment this week.

I checked into the hotel, then phoned Tom at his home to let him know I had arrived and would see him at the office in the morning. He was glad to have me back, he said. He had plans he needed to discuss with me. I wondered what that would be about.

I was tired. I hadn't slept more than a couple of hours since I'd gotten up Monday morning in Sint Maarten. With the four-hour time change, the clock radio in my room might have said eight-fifteen Tuesday evening but my body thought it was quarter past midnight. I stripped, had a shower and fell into bed, asleep in no more than a minute.

Tom wasn't expecting me early on Wednesday morning so I had breakfast in the restaurant before going back up to my room to read the paper and catch up on the news. At nine-thirty I left my room and walked the two blocks to Pinecone's office and took the elevator up to the fifth floor.

I walked into the familiar offices just before ten and startled Jenny, the receptionist.

"What are you doing here?" she asked in surprise. "I thought you were gone."

"I was ... and now I'm back," I grinned. "Tom's expecting me."

She was still a bit flustered but buzzed my boss and quickly told me to go to his office.

"Welcome back, Dex," Tom said enthusiastically, rising to greet me. "Good to see you. My god, man, you look like a million bucks. You've lost some weight too. Sint Maarten agreed with you," he smiled.

"It certainly did. In more ways than one."

Over the next hour, I filled him in on both the project and my personal life. I showed him a picture of the twins and myself that I carried around with me. He was impressed and said he envied me. He handed me a statement with my 2500 shares and their current value as of last year's audit. He also gave me a statement on my reserved salary over the time I was in the Caribbean. It surprised me. He had not reduced it to what he would normally pay a site engineer.

"Tom, this is very generous but I can't accept it. I didn't earn it so I'd feel guilty taking this from you. I didn't spend much while I was down there so I'm not out of pocket for anything. Just adjust it to what you would pay normally."

"Dex, you did a hell of job down there and Wolf and I have a plan that you are going to be a big part of if you want to. That salary will seem small compared to what we have planned. Interested?"

"Of course. I'd be crazy not to be," I said, confused about what he might have in mind.

"What do you plan to do about your personal life, Dex?" Tom asked later that afternoon.

"Well I won't be reconciling with Sandra, that's for sure. I'll file for divorce but on my own terms. I'm still not willing to reward her for her deceit. I won't leave her with nothing but I'm not in a very generous mood to be honest. I'll sign the house over to her and I'll make some other gestures to keep her from being penniless, but that's it."

"I'm still dumbfounded at what she did," Tom said. "It went so completely against who I thought she was."

"I feel the same way. The only thing I can think of is that she got bored with me and decided she needed someone more exciting. According to my friends, the twins, women can get that way if they aren't feeling good about how they look, or if they're afraid of getting old. If that's what it was then she couldn't have been looking in the mirror. Sandra was, and I'm sure still is, a very attractive woman."

"Well, I'm just glad Toni doesn't feel that way," Tom said of his wife. "I guess some women are a little more secure than others."

I nodded, wondering if Sandra would tell me what precipitated her affair. It wouldn't change anything but at least I'd know.

"So I take it you want me to hang onto the shares until the divorce settlement is done?"

"Yes please, Tom. I don't know what to expect from her so let's just leave things as they are until everything is finalized and signed off."

We parted company just before four that afternoon and I walked back to the hotel feeling fatigued. It had been an intense but exciting day and I wanted to think about what it might mean.

The late lunch meant I wasn't hungry and after a nap in my room, I headed across to a department store and started putting together a new wardrobe. Tom was right, I had lost weight so I might as well start from scratch and get new clothes. Two hours later I had a good supply of casual wear, underwear and socks. Tomorrow, I would hit the men's shops in the Granville Mall and find some suits, jackets, slacks and shoes.

I didn't know how to contact Sandra so I tried Merry's number. It had changed and the person answering didn't know her new number. Then my brain kicked in. If she couldn't sell the house then it was likely she was still living there. I punched in our old home phone number and it was picked up after two rings.

"Hello?" There wasn't much doubt it was Sandra.

"Hello, Sandra, it's Dex."

"Oh ... this is a surprise. I didn't expect to hear from you again."

She sounded cool ... not flustered at all.

"Yes, I'm back in Vancouver. I think we should get together and talk."

"Yes, I guess we should. When? Where?"

"I assume you are working so will Saturday be all right?"

"Yes. Where do you want to meet?"

"Are you living in the new house?"

"Yes. Merry and I live here now. What time?"

"Tomorrow afternoon. Say, two o'clock?"

"Yes. Two o'clock. That's fine."

There was no warmth or emotion in her voice. It was like talking to someone I had never met before.

"I'll see you then, Sandra. Good night."

I hung up without waiting for a reply. I wasn't going to leave her thinking that everything was going to be all right. It wasn't. I wasn't looking forward to tomorrow afternoon but it was something that had to be done and the sooner the better.

I didn't sleep very well that night. I imagine it was because I was dreading the meeting with my soon-to-be ex-wife. And if Meredith was there, would that complicate things, making them more difficult. It was a factor I hadn't counted on. At least I knew her mother had told her the truth about our separation.

I rented a car on Saturday morning and drove out to Maple Ridge. The new bridge had just been completed across the Fraser River and the new Pitt River crossing was well underway. The town was still growing, and signs of new construction and redevelopment were everywhere. It wasn't the sleepy little village in the country that it once was.

I had lunch at the pub we used to frequent but I saw no one I knew. Just as well. I was killing time until I would drive to the "new house" we had bought just before I left. I was still worrying over what kind of reception I would get.

I walked up the steps and rang the doorbell a few minutes before two. It was a habit of mine to be a bit early for appointments. The door opened immediately and I saw a different Sandra standing there, uncertainty in her eyes and actions.

"Hello, Sandra. May I come in?"

"Of course," she said, stepping aside. There was no attempt to embrace me and certainly no warmth in her voice.

I walked past her into the living room and found a chair to sit on. Sandra moved to a nearby chair and not the sofa as I had expected.

"You've been gone quite a while. By the look of you it was somewhere sunny," she said.

Her voice was unemotional and it matched her appearance. Neither a smile nor a frown, expressionless eyes, rigid posture, still hands and a flat tone of voice. She looked older, much older than her forty-five years. Whatever she had been going through in the past eighteen months hadn't been good for her.

"I'm back but I'm not sure for how long," I said. "I had no intention of staying around here and going through the agony of a divorce and watching my life destroyed before my eyes."

"Just leaving and running away didn't solve anything," she said.

"You're wrong. It was extremely good for my health, both mental and physical. I completely forgot about you and Randall and what you did to me."

"You really hate me, don't you," she said sadly.

"I certainly don't love you. What was I supposed to think when I read those e-mails? You didn't just commit adultery, you planned to take every dollar you could from me. How would you expect me to feel when I discovered that?"

She didn't answer.

"I have a proposal for you. I'm willing to grant you a divorce but on my terms. Under the circumstances, I think my offer is fair. I'd like you to look it over and if you agree, I'll have it drawn up by a lawyer and you can sign it and it will be all over."

I passed her the typed sheet and she looked at it.

"I'm entitled to half our assets. This doesn't give me half," she said, still showing little emotion.

"I have several e-mails that describe your conspiring with Randall to extract more than fifty percent from me. How do you think a judge would view that? And what about Randall abandoning his family. Do you think a judge would reward you for that?

"As I said, I think my offer is fair but it's your choice. Turn it down and the situation stays as it is. You live in this house because I allow it. It's in my name, not yours. You might want to think about that. I'll call you next week for an answer. I suggest you think carefully before you make a decision."

I sat quietly as she continued to look at the paper in her hand but I sensed she wasn't reading the words any longer.

"Can you tell me why?" I asked finally.

She looked up and again I was struck by just how much her appearance had changed.

"I don't really know," she said at length. "I suppose I was at an age when I wasn't sure of myself. How I looked. Was I desirable any more? I don't remember you saying I was. When Randall began to … seduce me … I was flattered. It felt good. I guess I let my emotions overrule my brain. I knew it was wrong but I was excited and he was a powerful lover. It all seemed so simple after a while. We would get a divorce from our spouses and live happily ever after. I had no idea that it was all a scam."

"A scam?"

"Yes. He had no intention of marrying me. Apparently he was skimming money from the accounts of elderly clients thinking they wouldn't realize what was happening. Unfortunately, one of the clients' sons realized what was going on and blew the whistle. I don't know how many hours I spent answering questions about what I knew and where the money was.

"They were going to charge me with conspiracy to defraud but the Crown Prosecutor decided not to because they weren't sure of a conviction. That was after I agreed to tell them everything I knew … which wasn't much. Randall kept all of this to himself. I had no idea he was stealing money from those people."

"So I take it Randall is being charged?" I said.

"Yes but I don't know what with. Something about breach of fiduciary duty and theft I think. I probably won't be called as a witness at his trial they said. Needless to say, it hasn't done my reputation any good."

"A pretty high price for sex don't you think?"

"Yes … a very high price. My husband, my self respect, my job," she said, looking at me once again. "I'm sorry, Dex. I wish I had it to do all over again … but I don't. All I can say is … I'm sorry."

"I'll call you Wednesday," I repeated as I rose and walked to the door, letting myself out.

It was a much shorter meeting than I had planned but Sandra had been so defeated that I didn't feel brow-beating her into a confession was necessary. She understood what she had done wrong and it at least elicited an apology.

As I drove back to the city, I tried to understand what might have caused our marriage to dissolve the way it had. Was she bored and needed some excitement? Was I lacking in bed in some way? The twins didn't think so. I went around and around on the subject and came to no conclusion. Whatever the reason, it had happened and I had made a decision I didn't intend to change. I would live my life without Sandra no matter what she decided about the divorce.

Chapter 5
The Next Step

Typically, Tom Yardley and I were the first two people in the office each morning. Tom was an early riser by nature, and always anxious to get to work first thing. I was similar because I was at my best in the morning and that was when I did my most effective work. So it was no surprise that when I arrived at the Pinecone office on Monday morning Tom was already there, pouring his first cup of coffee. I joined him.

"Good morning, Dex. Ready to get back to work?"

"Yes, but I guess that does bring up the question about Dorothy. I don't want to hurt her and I hear she did a great job while I was away. I was thinking maybe another site-rep assignment."

"Well, I suppose we could do that but I think you should hold on until later this morning. I'd like you to get up to speed with Dorothy on the department then meet me here in my office at ten o'clock. I have something that might interest you."

"Okay ... fine, ten o'clock. I take it there's no point in my asking what the meeting's about?" I grinned.

"None at all. See you then," he said with a smile.

When I walked into Tom's office at ten that morning I was surprised to see Wolf Balak sitting in a comfortable chair, enjoying a coffee.

"Hey, Wolf. How are you? Long time no see."

"I am good, Dex. Good to see you too. I hear good things about you on our airport job," he said in his thick German accent.

"Oh … from whom?"

"The contractor. He said he would work with Pinecone anytime in the future. He thought you were very professional and handled any problems quickly. Thank you for that," he smiled.

"To tell the truth, Wolf, we didn't have very many problems. That job went about as smoothly as any we've ever had. A little slowly, perhaps, but pretty smoothly."

He nodded. "It is good to have one like that, especially when it is in a foreign country."

"The reason I asked you to join us, Dex," Tom interrupted, "is that we have a proposal to put to you."

That got my immediate attention.

It was Wolf who opened the discussion.

"You will not be aware that Tom and I have been negotiating with another company to buy controlling interest in them. We want to expand our business and this is the quickest way to accomplish that. The company that we want to acquire is Trent Engineering in Toronto. They have fallen on hard times and need an injection of business activity to get back to where they once were."

"Trent was, once upon a time, one of the most respected small firms in Canada," Tom continued. "Unfortunately, the senior partners either retired or expired. What they had left were competent engineers but with no drive to find new business. Their opportunities have been dwindling steadily over this recent declining economy and we were able to acquire a 55% share of ownership for an attractive price."

"You know how much I like to find new opportunities," Wolf went on. "I pride myself in my engineering skill but the truth is that I am a better salesman. So … now we have this new addition to the Pinecone family and we need your help."

I sat looking at them. This was an unexpected surprise. I couldn't guess what Tom and Wolf wanted from me since I didn't know anything about Trent Engineering.

"We're not in a position to compete with the big civil engineering firms like SNC-Lavalin or Hatch but we sit well in our slot," Tom said. "We've been successful because we stick with what we know best and spend a lot of time with architects and construction companies to make sure they are confident with us. It's been a good strategy and we plan to maintain it."

"How do I fit in?" I asked.

"When the acquisition is complete in the next month," Tom went on, "we'll want you to go to Toronto and assess the capabilities there. There's been a freeze on spending over the last three years and I know how much we've spent on updating our programs and equipment so I'm expecting they'll need to catch up. We want the same programs at both offices, naturally."

"That makes sense," I said. "I won't know until I get there how long I'll need. How many operators do they have?"

"I think I saw about two dozen work stations," Wolf answered. "Not all of them were occupied but, if we can revitalize the company, you would want that many at least."

"We have nearly thirty here," I noted. "Is there room for expansion?"

"Not really. We might move the engineering and executive staff to another floor if that were necessary. We will leave it up to you to decide," Wolf said.

"Okay … so you want me in Toronto when?"

"March 15th," Tom responded. "Any problem with that?"

"No … none. I assume I'll have some accommodation available?"

"Yes. There's a suites residence a block from the office. Both Wolf and I have stayed there and it's fine. Naturally, all your expenses will be covered. Cost of acquisition you know," Tom grinned.

"Okay then. Anything else?" I asked.

"Yes. Your title and salary will change. You are now Vice President, Design Services, Pinecone-Trent Engineering. It will be effective March 1st. I've already ordered the business cards," Tom grinned again.

"Wow. Another thing I didn't expect. Thank you very much. You were pretty sure I would take this assignment, I guess."

"Well, considering your situation, I thought it wouldn't cause a problem. Maybe I shouldn't have taken that for granted," Tom admitted.

"No problem. I'm better off being busy and somewhere other than here for the time being. We can always talk about the future when I've figured out what I want from my life. By the way, I'll be filing for divorce if Sandra accepts my proposal. I'll know in a couple of days. If she turns it down I'll just go on as before until I can wear her down."

"I am very sorry to hear of your problem, Dex," Wolf said sadly. "It must be very hard to accept what Sandra has done after all these years. I was delighted with the job you did for us in Sint Maarten. I think for you, it was very good therapy, yes?"

"Yes, it was. I think Toronto could be more of the same. I hope so, anyway."

"How is your relationship with your son and daughter now?" Tom asked.

"Okay now. They know the truth and understand why I did what I did. Meredith is very disappointed that there isn't any hope of reconciliation and she is still close to her mother. They are living together at our house for now. Jon is working in Chile and understands completely. He has no illusions about his mother and me."

"And Sandra?" Tom asked.

"You would be shocked if you saw her, I think. She's aged and doesn't seem to have much life in her. I know she understands what she's done and that there is no going back but she doesn't seem to be able to move on from it. I saw her on Saturday and it was a very short, unemotional meeting with very little accomplished as far as I was concerned. However, we'll see what happens when I ask for an answer on my settlement proposal."

"Alright, Dex," Tom sighed. "We wish you luck. Oh, by the way, Dorothy is aware of this meeting. I wanted her to be confident she wasn't about to lose her job when you returned. You're still her boss, though."

"Easiest person I ever supervised," I smiled. "You mind if I take her to lunch today? I'd like to let her know what's happening."

"No problem," Tom responded. "She's aware of the acquisition and knows not to talk about it. I told her I would be discussing it with you too so it won't come as a surprise."

I ended the meeting feeling quite light-headed. A vice presidency! I never expected that. I didn't even bother to ask about the salary. I was sure Tom and Wolf would treat me fairly. This was a very good boost for my morale. I had a new project and a new responsibility.

I stopped by Dorothy's desk.

"Do you have time for lunch today, Dorothy?"

"Yes, I guess so," she answered tentatively. She was obviously curious about my request and I was glad that Tom had told her that her job was secure.

"Why don't I come and get you about twelve-thirty and we'll head for Gassy Jack's. You don't have anything urgent for the rest of the day, do you?"

"No. I'm caught up. I'll see you then."

The restaurant was thinning out by the time we arrived, and the noise level had dropped from its usual loud level during the early lunch hour. The brokerage boys had come and gone before noon, and we were able to find a table in a corner where it wouldn't be too near other patrons.

"I wanted to thank you for doing such a great job since I've been gone, Dorothy. I know Tom told you about what's happening so we can talk about it if you like. You'll still report to me since they've decided to appoint me V.P. Design Services. I'm heading for Toronto in a couple of weeks to bring them up to speed with what we are doing. I want them running as well as Vancouver is when I'm done. I'll be on the lookout for another Dorothy," I smiled.

"Thank you, Dex. I really appreciate your support. I love the job and all the staff have been great about my taking over."

"Good, I'm glad to hear that. I don't know what's needed in Toronto yet but I'll be in contact with you probably daily to match up what we are doing here with what we need there. I've been out of the loop for eighteen months so I'm sure things have changed."

The waitress arrived and we ordered our lunch. Dorothy Milner was a thirty-something young lady, married, no children, attractive dark brown hair, nice build, well dressed. She was my vision of a well-balanced career woman. Very professional on the job without losing her femininity.

"I hope I'm not out of line, Dex, but I was very sorry to hear about you and your wife. That must have been hard for you."

"It was. The best thing that happened was that Sint Maarten airport job. It got me away from here and out of my discomfort zone," I kidded. "I met some interesting people down there that helped distract me."

"Oh … some interesting female people?" she grinned.

"Yeah. A pair of twins," I said, pulling the picture out of my wallet.

"Oh, wow!" Dorothy remarked when she saw them. "Hot looking babes, Dex. Very hot!"

"Yes, indeed. Made this old codger sit up and take notice."

"Old codger? You must be kidding. Have you looked at yourself since you got back? Tanned, fit. Hell, Dex, you're now a certified hunk. If I wasn't happily married, I'd be after you," she giggled.

"Thanks. I have to admit, I feel a lot better and several people have noticed and said something. It does help lift one's spirits."

"I have a couple of single girlfriends that would jump at the chance to date you. You want me to give them your phone number? I wouldn't do this for just anyone. Only someone I trust."

"No … no … not just yet. I'm hoping I can get my situation with Sandra resolved this week, then maybe I can think about dating."

She nodded. "I understand. But remember, if you ever need a date I can get you one like that!" she said, snapping her fingers.

"You sure know how to make a guy feel good, Dorothy."

We had a leisurely lunch and walked back to the office just before two o'clock. It was good to reconnect with Dorothy again. She was going to be an important cog in the Vancouver office for some years to come. She was happy in her job and did it very well. I'm told she had a firm hand on the staff but that they all supported her.

Tuesday evening my cell phone chirped and instead of ignoring it I decided to answer it.

"Hi, Daddy, it's me, Merry," my daughter announced.

"Hello, Sweetheart. How are you? It's great to hear from you."

"I know I should have called sooner. I just realized you probably didn't have my cell phone number."

"No … I figured I could call you at the house. I wasn't sure how anxious you were to talk to me," I admitted.

"Daddy, you don't have to worry about that. I understand why you were so upset but I can't abandon Mom just now. She's really down about what's happened. I'm afraid she's depressed so I want to be close to her and help her."

"I think that's very good of you, Merry. I'm glad your mother has someone to look out for her."

"Daddy, I called because I wanted you to know that I've been talking to Mom about your settlement offer. I've told her she should accept it and move on. I don't think it's a good thing for this to drag on for ever and ever. It won't do her any good … I mean emotionally. She has to accept that she did something very wrong and she shouldn't expect to be rewarded for that. I think I've got through to her but I guess you'll know for sure when you talk to her tomorrow night."

"Thank you, Merry. I appreciate your effort. I hope she takes your advice. I don't want to hurt her any more either but I've drawn a line in the sand about this issue and she has to accept that I'm not going to argue back and forth about it."

"I know, Daddy. I wish it never happened, but … both of you need to get on with your lives. You've seen the way she looks. I think Jon would be sick if he saw her now. She needs to find something to get her back to the land of the living."

"You've done all you can, Merry. You are a wonderful daughter and I'm sure your mother knows that. You make me very proud to be your father."

I could hear a sniffle at the other end of the line and, to be honest, I wasn't far from tears either.

"Good night, Daddy. We'll talk soon."

After I'd closed my phone I realized I hadn't told her about my promotion and leaving for Toronto in a couple of weeks. Time enough for that later this week I suppose.

By the time Wednesday evening rolled around I was very antsy about Sandra's decision. I really wanted this whole ugly affair to be over with. There wasn't going to be a reconciliation and I wasn't, in my opinion, out for blood. I just wanted a fair settlement to the divorce; one that allowed me to hold my head up despite the fact that she had cuckolded me in my own back yard.

"Hello, Sandra. I called to get your answer on my settlement proposal."

I wasn't about to beat around the bush or engage in pointless small talk.

"Yes, Dex," she answered with a sigh. "Merry has convinced me that your proposal is fair, so I will sign the documents on that basis. I'm not sure that I'm really getting what I should but I suppose that's the price I have to pay for what I did."

"I think you've made a good decision, Sandra. Both of us have to move on with our lives even though they will be separate. I'll have some good memories despite how it all ended. I'll try hard to wipe away the bad ones."

"Yes … I think that's the best thing. No point in dwelling on the mistakes. How do you want to handle this?"

"I've already had my lawyer draw up the proposal so I'll send it to your lawyer and you can arrange a meeting for the four of us to sign."

"All right. Did Merry tell you that we want to put the house up for sale?"

"No, but that makes sense. Both of you are working downtown so finding a place closer would make your life easier. I'll sign the house over to you as agreed."

"We're thinking of buying a condo at False Creek. We could walk to work from there."

"Good. I'm glad Merry is staying close with you. I think that will be good for both of you for the next little while."

"Yes … she's been a tower of strength for me. I really don't know what I would have done without her. I just hope she finds a guy one of these days. I don't want her giving up her life to look after me."

"I agree. Well, that's something you can help her with. I'm sure she'll recognize it when you're back to your normal self," I said optimistically.

We talked for a few minutes more about how the sale and distribution of assets would take place before we ended the call.

I took the elevator down to the lounge on the main floor and ordered a double scotch and soda. It took a second one to relax me enough to feel that I'd just about come to the end of the road in terms of our marriage. Now it was a matter of signing some documents and filing the divorce papers. In six months I would be a single man once more.

I was glad I'd called it a night after just the two drinks and gone to bed early. I don't think I really understood how stressed I was over the divorce and settlement issues.

I woke up at my usual time and went through my morning routine before taking the elevator to the lobby and the restaurant. I had my usual light breakfast before walking to the office on what was another drizzly, wet, grey morning in Vancouver. Sint Maarten had spoiled me.

The next two weeks seemed to crawl by as I spent my time with Dorothy going over the new upgrades that had been installed on the server while I was away, plus the equipment changes that were on her wish list. We took a couple of days to have suppliers demonstrate their new wares, especially plotters and modeling software. I had to come to a decision about what to recommend for both operations now but I was working blind as far as Toronto went.

Finally, on Sunday morning, March 14, I boarded an Air Canada flight to Toronto for my next "adventure." I suppose I was feeling pretty confident as I thought about the challenge before me. Hadn't everything gone according to plan in Sint Maarten? I had a good idea of what we wanted to do in Toronto and the only unknown was the quality of the people on hand.

I checked into the Rossmoor Suites and found they had reserved a two-bedroom unit for me that was really a compact, fully furnished apartment. It was more than I would need for my stay. On top of that the building facilities included a fitness centre, a billiards room, virtual golf and a theatre room. If I needed space for an out-of-office meeting, rooms were available for that as well. I was more than satisfied with the modern facility.

Following my usual habits I prepared to be in the Trent offices just after seven on Monday morning. When I arrived I found the office dark and the door locked. Note to self: obtain a key. I recalled seeing a coffee shop off the lobby of the building and headed down to see if I could ascertain when the office opened.

The middle-aged waitress asked for my order and I chose a latté.

"Do you know when the offices open at Trent Engineering?" I asked when she delivered my coffee.

"Trent? That's on the seventh floor?"

I nodded.

"Eight o'clock for the worker bees. The big boys usually don't show up until nine."

"Thanks," I said, thinking I had some adjusting to do. This was Toronto not Vancouver. Hours of work were later, both starting and finishing. However, I didn't see any reason not to be the first person in the office if that's what helped me do my job well. I wouldn't force the staff to follow my example but I wondered how many might take my habits to be a good model for themselves. After all, it would allow them to leave earlier too. No reason the office couldn't have staggered work hours, I thought.

I nursed my latté until just before eight o'clock and headed for the elevators once more. The traffic had increased substantially and a number of people had come into the coffee shop to get a hot drink or a pastry to go before heading to their offices. I took the crowded elevator to the seventh floor and several people got off at the same time. I waited before following them into the Trent offices.

The receptionist was just fixing her headset in place as I stood before her.

"Good morning, I'm Dexter McLeod. I believe I'm expected," I said politely.

"Oh … uhhhmmm … I don't have any note here about that. Do you know who you are supposed to see?"

"Mr. John Flannery."

"Oh … well … Mr. Flannery isn't usually in until nine o'clock. Would you like to wait?"

"I guess I'd better," I smiled. "I'm supposed to be working here for the next few weeks." I handed her my card.

"Oh … Mr. McLeod. You're from Vancouver. Why don't I call Mr. Flannery on his cell phone and find out where he is. I'm sure he's expecting you."

"That's very kind of you. Thank you," I said with a smile. Never upset the receptionist was a golden rule of mine.

She dialed a number and waited for a few seconds.

"Mr. Flannery, it's Brigit at the office. There's a Mr. McLeod from Vancouver here to see you."

I couldn't hear the other end of the conversation but I gather it wasn't pleasant if the frown on young Brigit's face was any indication.

"Yes, sir, I'll tell him," she said finally.

"I'm sorry Mr. McLeod. Mr. Flannery won't be in until nine o'clock. He suggested you might want to have a coffee and wait here in the lobby for him."

She looked embarrassed and I felt for her. She was the messenger and Flannery was obviously one of the senior executives.

"Who is Mr. Flannery?" I asked.

"He's the senior partner. Mr. Golowitz and Mr. Zarek are the other partners. They will be here at nine this morning as well. I'm sorry no one was here to greet you, sir."

"Please, call me Dex. Everyone does. I'm here to modernize the design department."

"I don't think Mr. Flannery would be very happy with me if I was too familiar with one of our vice presidents," she said seriously.

"Well okay then, but when no one else is around it's Dex and Brigit, right?"

She smiled and agreed. One on my side, I thought. I was now alerted that perhaps the senior people were not quite as enthusiastic about the acquisition as I might have been led to believe. I cautioned myself not to jump to conclusions and wait and see what happened.

Just before nine, a large, imposing man of some sixty-plus years entered the office, looked me over once and turned to Brigit. She handed him some message slips and he looked at them casually. Finally, he turned to me.

"Are you McLeod?" he asked in a no-nonsense tone.

"Dexter McLeod, Mr. Flannery," I said standing and holding out my hand.

He ignored it. "I've got some things to do first thing this morning. I'll let you know when I have time to see you," he snorted, turning his back on me and walking away to the back of the offices.

I was stunned. What the fuck was this? I turned to Brigit and she was red-faced but shrugged as she took another call.

I had another hour before Tom would be in the office so I would bide my time. I wasn't about to pull rank but I wasn't going to be treated like a second-class citizen by some eastern stuffed shirt. He needed to be reminded who owned the majority of this business but not by me.

As the clock struck ten, Flannery had still not shown his face, so I approached the reception desk and handed Brigit another of my cards.

"If Mr. Flannery should decide to grace me with his presence, tell him he can contact me on my cell. The number is on the card. Thank you, Brigit."

I turned and walked toward the door to the elevators.

"Mr. McLeod," Brigit called after me. I turned. "I'm sorry, sir." I nodded.

That young lady was a keeper. Flannery on the other hand was really pissing me off. I headed for the washroom I saw off the elevators. It was empty so it would serve my purpose.

"Tom Yardley," he answered.

"You bastard!" I spat.

I heard his outburst of laughter as he recognized my voice.

"I take it you've met the esteemed Mr. Flannery," he said, barely able to contain himself.

"Not really. He waltzed into the office at nine o'clock, told me he'd see me when he had time, said I could wait for him in the lobby, then disappeared. I still haven't heard from him."

"I should have warned you, Dex. He's miserable old man. He's convinced that we stole the company from him. The other three minority partners were all for the deal but Flannery was convinced the business just needed some capital and everything would be all right. He and Wolf had a real ding-dong when the final deal was proposed but Flannery lost because we had the shares of the other three partners and he was screwed."

"Three? I thought there was just two besides Flannery."

"No … one of the widows of another partner had shares that tipped the balance. She's not active in the firm but is interested in seeing it restored to its former glory."

"And you couldn't see yourself to warn me about this," I said, not altogether happy with my boss.

"Sorry, Dex. I didn't want to pollute the water before you even got there. I will call Mr. Flannery with whom I have at least a civil relationship and tell him that you are not to be treated in this manner. He doesn't need the problems we can cause if he keeps up with this attitude."

"Thanks, Tom. I'll cool it for now but you'd better give me someone else to work with. I don't think I could stomach much of Flannery on a regular basis."

"Okay. He'll probably be relieved to remove you from his sight. I knew he wasn't going to be pleasant and I guess I owe you one from dropping you in it. My apologies."

"All right, Tom. I have a feeling this job isn't going to go quite as nicely as my last one. I hope I'm wrong."

"Dex, you can handle it. I've watched you with your people for years. You'll figure it out. Call me if Flannery gives you any more trouble."

"Okay. I'd better get back to the office before *His Majesty* reports me absent without leave."

Tom laughed again and that was the end of our conversation.

Chapter 6
Smoothing the Waters

It was almost 10:20 when Mr. Flannery decided to make an appearance. He looked decidedly unhappy when he strode out of his hideaway and marched up to my chair in the reception area.

"I'll see you now, Mr. McLeod," he snarled and immediately turned and stomped back from where he came.

I turned and looked at Brigit and saw her shake her head with a look of dismay. I pushed myself up out of the chair and followed Flannery. His office was in the far corner of the floor with windows on two walls overlooking the city and the lakefront. He pointed to a chair at one corner of his desk and I sat.

"So what are you here for?" Flannery began without the slightest hint of politeness.

"Are you telling me you haven't been informed of the purpose of my visit?" I was all set to go one on one with him if he pushed his attitude much more.

His head came up and his eyes narrowed. I don't think he quite expected me to confront him.

"There was some mention of a visit by one of the Vancouver people," he said, offering nothing more.

"I find that hard to believe. I talked to Tom Yardley a few minutes ago. I'm sure he told you what the object of my visit was. Is there some reason you object to my presence?" I was working hard to keep my voice even and controlled.

"I object to the theft of my company by a bunch of western upstarts. There's nothing you have to offer Trent Engineering that we can't do ourselves," he snarled.

"Mr. Flannery, I'm here to upgrade your CADD systems and bring them in line with the Pinecone systems. I'd be very disappointed if you're telling me I can't expect the cooperation of your staff."

"You'll get your cooperation, Mr. McLeod. Just make sure you don't interfere with the work we have on hand. We have deadlines to meet and I expect them to be met regardless of your little project."

I tried to stare him down but he was reluctant to look me in the eye.

"Who will I be working with in the CADD department?" I asked.

"Whoever can spare the time," he said dismissively. "You'll have to work that out yourself."

"I'd like an office as well," I said, struggling to keep my temper.

"You'll have to make do with whatever you can find."

"Are we finished here?" I asked, beginning to rise. I wanted out of this office as soon as I could.

"Yes," was all I got from him in response.

I walked out to the reception desk and flopped into the chair I had previously occupied. I needed to cool off before I said or did something I would regret. Brigit looked at me and I think I was pretty easy to read.

"Don't be too upset, Mr. McLeod. He's been very unhappy these last few months. He's been nasty to just about everyone," she said apologetically.

"Thank you, Brigit. By the way, do you know if there are any unused offices available, preferable in the design area?"

"Oh yes, we have three. If you wait until lunch hour, I'll show you around and you can decide which one is best for you."

"Thank you again. I'm grateful for your help."

I went down to the café in the lobby at 11:30 and ordered a sandwich and a tomato juice to go. I didn't want to cut into Brigit's lunch hour any more than necessary.

"Where do you and the staff eat lunch, Brigit?" I asked when I returned.

"There's an area in the back that's not being used and we put some chairs and tables in there. Some people go out to lunch but a lot of us go there or eat at our desks. I can't do that, naturally."

"Mind if I join you?"

"No ... of course not. It might be a chance for you to meet some of the people."

The more I was around Brigit the more I liked her attitude. I had a hunch I was going to need all the friends I could find in this job.

Just after noon I followed Brigit to the so-called lunch area. I noticed it was about as far from Flannery's office as you could get. It was an open space of about 500 sq. ft., with a collection of unmatched chairs and tables scattered about the room. There was no sink but a rather ancient microwave was sitting on one table and an old refrigerator was standing in a nearby corner. Not exactly what I would describe as a lunch room.

Brigit guided me to a table near a window and we sat. There was room for another four people at this table but so far no one had approached. A couple of minutes later another young woman entered the room, saw Brigit and waved while walking directly to our table.

"Hi, Brigit," she said brightly, giving me the once-over.

"Hi Petra. This is Dexter McLeod. He's going to be working with us for a while."

I stood and shook the young woman's hand. "Nice to meet you, Petra. You can call me Dex. What do you do here?"

"I'm in the design department. Slaving away in front of a computer screen all day," she grinned.

I took a card from my shirt pocket and passed it to her.

"Looks like we'll be spending some time together then," I said. "I'm here to update the CADD systems and equipment. Bring you up to the latest standards."

"Oh, wonderful! That's great to hear," she enthused, looking at my card. I saw her eyes widen as she read the card.

"What are you doing here?" she asked. "I mean in this place. Shouldn't you be with the other managers?"

I shook my head and I could see a big grin on Brigit's face.

"Nope. I'm happy with the people I work with. I'd like to have that kind of relationship with your department."

"Well … that'll be different," Petra said with a wrinkled brow. "Most of the senior people don't mix with us peons."

"I was a peon for many years, Petra. I don't forget where I came from and don't be fooled by the vice president title. It's new and shiny and unused. Around my office in Vancouver, everyone calls me Dex. We don't stand on formality."

"I'd get fired or maybe shot if I didn't call all the senior people, Mister," she said. "This place is pretty 'old-school' in my opinion."

"I've only met Mr. Flannery so far but I can see where that idea comes from."

Both women giggled at my comment but didn't offer any reinforcement.

A couple of minutes later, a short dark-haired man joined us at the table.

"Mr. McLeod, this is Carlo de Prata, also one of our CADD operators."

"Hi, Carlo, Dexter McLeod," I said, handing him one of my cards.

He looked at it and like Petra, his eyebrows raised and he looked at me.

"Uh … nice to meet you, sir," he said uncertainly.

"Relax Carlo. It's Dex to most of the people around here. I'm here to bring the systems up to date on both software and hardware."

"Oh … good … I've been hoping something would happen when we heard that there'd been a take-over," he said with an obvious sigh of relief.

"Well, it's not exactly a take-over. Pinecone are partners with Trent Engineering now. Our job is to help you grow back to what you once were and more. It looks like we might need more than just computers and software, though. You could use a proper lunch room."

"Wouldn't that be nice," Petra said, with Brigit nodding.

"I'll see what I can do," I said with a smile. "In the meantime, I need a guide to take me around the design department. Any volunteers?" I grinned.

"I'm probably the best one to do that," Petra said. "I've been here the longest after Terry Sanderson. He's the senior man in our department."

"Maybe I should meet with Terry then so I don't ruffle any feathers," I suggested.

"No problem. I'll go get him and we can talk," she said, rising to walk to another table. She bent over near a big redheaded man and said a few words. He turned to look at me then nodded to Petra and stood.

"Mr. McLeod, this is Terry Sanderson, senior operator."

I stood and shook hands with him. He was a large, friendly, freckle-faced man in his forties I guessed.

"Nice to meet you, Terry. I'm Dex," I said, handing him my card.

"Yes, I've been expecting someone. Nice to see you're here so quickly. I understand you'd like a tour."

"If you've got the time. I don't want to interrupt anything important."

"Not a problem. I've finished my lunch so we can go anytime you're ready," he said.

"Ladies, if you'll excuse me, duty calls," I smiled. "Nice meeting you, Petra. Oh, and Brigit, do you know where I can get a key to the office?"

"Yes," she said, "but you won't like my answer. Only Mr. Flannery can authorize that. Sorry."

I nodded. "Okay, I'll find a way. Lead on, Terry," I said, hiding my irritation at the roadblocks I seemed to be encountering so early in my stay. Another thing to talk to Tom about, I thought. I'd better start writing this down. The list was getting longer and I'd only been here a couple of hours.

Terry gave me a comprehensive tour of the twenty-station CADD room. There were twelve active units, symptomatic of the decline in their business. He admitted that some of the unused units had been cannibalized for parts or software when problems arose. They had no budget for anything short of essential repairs.

Terry was candid but careful in his comments. He admitted he was hopeful that the merger would bring the equipment and software up to date but didn't expect to have it happen this quickly. He said it would be a big boost to the morale of the people in the office. I was glad to hear that. That should put a few more staff on my side.

Brigit had shown me the open offices and I found one just where I wanted it with easy access to the department but private enough when it was required. I put my laptop down on the desk, pulled out an Ethernet cable and hooked into the wall outlet. Within seconds, I was confronted with a gateway that required a password. Good. There was some security in place.

Terry gave me the password for the week and I set up my station, logging on after registering. I spent the next hour surfing the site and seeing what we were working with. There was a job log and I reviewed that to see what our people were working on. It wasn't a very long list.

The sooner I got this department up to speed, the sooner I could turn Wolf loose on the potential clients.

At five o'clock I called Tom once more, having written a list of things I needed to resolve … or work around.

"I can't even get a key to the office without Flannery's approval. Doesn't he delegate anything? Who's the second in command?" I asked.

"The two junior partners are active engineers and you should make their acquaintance. In the meantime, borrow a key from someone and make a copy. I'll cover for you if it's necessary. I doubt it will be. Flannery was never there before nine and very seldom after four."

"Jesus, Tom. No wonder the business is in trouble."

"It isn't that simple, Dex. Flannery's wife has contracted MS and I think that's contributed to his problems. It's one thing to have the business shrink, it's another to try and deal with an ill wife. This is not public knowledge, Dex. I got the information from Michelle Gauthier."

"Who is she?"

"The minority fourth partner. Her husband was a real go-getter and when he died unexpectedly, the aggressive hunt for new work died with him. The rest of the people there are pretty much stay-at-home engineers."

"Can you give me a breakdown of who owns what shares, or is that top secret?"

"Nope, it's not secret, although I wouldn't want it to become common knowledge. In the total structure, Pinecone owns 55% and Trent owns 45% of the outstanding shares. Inside Pinecone, Wolf and I own 40% each. The other 20% of Pinecone is made up of people like you.

"At Trent, Flannery owns 42%, the two junior partners own 20% each and Mrs. Gauthier owns the remaining 18%. It was the two junior partners and Mrs. Gauthier that made the merger possible. You already know how Flannery felt about that."

"I haven't met the other three yet. Should I?"

"Yes, particularly the two active partners. You know how hard we worked to get a good relationship between the engineers and the designers. I'd like to see that at Trent too."

"Yeah. I guess we've had it pretty good at Pinecone and haven't had to deal with this kind of problem. Well, I'll introduce myself to the engineering department tomorrow. I'll let you know how that goes.

"By the way, is there any wiggle room in my budget for a lunch room? These people have nothing here. The space is available but right now it's not very impressive."

"As long as you don't turn it into a luxury restaurant, go ahead. I'll circulate an e-mail authorizing that and other changes as required. Just keep me informed."

"Thanks, Tom. I feel a bit better. If I can get Flannery off my back I should be able to make some progress here fairly soon."

I put the phone down after we signed off and sighed. This was definitely going to be a challenge. I walked out of the office as Terry was packing up to go home and asked him if he had a key to the office.

"Sure. I don't use it very often but if you need it, just ask," he said.

"I'd like to borrow it and make a copy. I can get it back to you tomorrow."

"Did Flannery okay this?" he asked nervously.

"Nope, Tom Yardley did. Don't worry, if he kicks up a fuss he won't know I got it from you," I grinned.

Terry snorted a laugh and handed me the key. "Nice to see things changing, Dex."

I nodded. We were making progress already.

The next four days went by in a whoosh. I met with the company that provided IT service for Trent, getting their advice on reliable suppliers of hardware in the area. The IT rep, whom Terry had recommended, was quite surprised that we would ask his opinion. Not that other companies didn't, just that Trent had never asked.

I introduced myself to Rueben Golowitz and Dick Zarek, the senior engineers and shareholders. I got a pleasant reception and promised I would follow up with them in a week or so.

I did a station-by-station assessment of what we had on hand and it was discouraging to say the least. Band-Aid solutions were everywhere and the software was a mish-mash of dated programs. The only thing that seemed to be in reasonably decent shape was the server itself. It had expansion capability and I knew immediately that we would need it.

I was making a list of needs as I went and it was getting longer with each progressive step. On Friday afternoon I e-mailed my findings to Tom, hoping it wouldn't cause a meltdown in Vancouver when he saw it. I had a return phone call within thirty minutes.

"It's a good thing we put a big contingency in the budget, Dex. That list you've given me. Do you need all of it at once?" Tom asked.

"No, but this just covers the active work stations, Tom. They're only using twelve stations of the twenty available. We should fix those first, then add the others as the work picks up."

"Okay, you know best. Any more problems with Flannery?"

"No ... he's been invisible, thankfully. I don't think he ever comes into this department from what I've learned."

"Good ... just as well. So sit down with the procurement department on Monday and get this stuff ordered. You'll have my authorization by e-mail along with a copy to whomever you're working with."

I gave Tom the name of the head of procurement and her e-mail address. I was grateful for the swift approval of my request. It was one of those things that made it pleasant to work for him. He trusted me, didn't micro-manage and didn't dither. I also knew getting quick approval was an atypical action in larger companies.

I began holding meetings with all the design staff at 4:30 in the afternoon. My purpose was to keep them informed daily on what we were doing and why. I also wanted to ask for their opinions on a number of issues from the type of chairs we provided to the lunch room facilities. They were a pretty quiet bunch for the first two meetings but with a little coaching by Terry and Petra, the ice was broken and we began to get a lot of feedback.

I formed a lunch room committee to come up with a plan for the room and a budget. I didn't have any trouble getting volunteers. I formed another committee to decide on whether to introduce staggered work hours. Would some people like to start earlier and leave earlier? A third committee was struck to examine the work stations for possible improvements in the future.

By late Friday afternoon, I had the entire twelve design staffers onside and enthusiastic about what was going to happen. I also had a visit from Brigit, saying some of the girls in accounting and procurement, along with herself, would be happy to volunteer on any of the committees. That felt good as well.

Janice Meriwether was the manager of procurement, a veteran of provincial government service. She was easily in her fifties but a very active and motivated woman. Turning her loose on some projects would be fun to watch. I shocked her with the purchase order request for equipment and software along with the attached authorization.

"We couldn't get a pencil sharpened around here without Flannel-pants' approval," she said seriously.

I burst out laughing of course. So that was his nickname.

I'd also broken through the formality barrier. I was Dex and I addressed those people I came into contact with by their first names as well. It took most of the week for them to get used to it but again, it was another popular move.

When I opened my apartment door on Friday evening I was whipped. I'd compressed about two weeks work into one but I felt it was necessary for me to hit the ground running to impress upon the staff that this wasn't some quick-and-dirty exercise. We were here to make things happen and it may have been that the most significant thing I had done that week was to do something about the lunch room.

During the second week, I wanted to establish relations with the engineering staff. I didn't know what to expect because few of the people in my department had any contact with them on a personal basis. It was strictly business. I had other objectives. I sought out Janice Meriwether and invited her for coffee on Tuesday morning.

"I have a list of the engineers in our office but I haven't met any of them yet. Can you give me some idea of what to expect?"

I don't think she was ready for my question. I was asking her opinion on senior staff and I'm guessing that was "out of bounds" in the past.

She stumbled and stammered a bit but then I guess she decided I wasn't trying to trick her.

"You've already met Dick Zarek and Rueben Golowitz, the senior men. Both are good guys who tolerate Flannery. I understand they welcomed the merger. No surprise there. Why do you want to know?"

I explained the relationship between the designers and engineers in our Vancouver office and I saw her nodding approval as I spoke.

"I think they'd welcome that. The old regime here had a pretty rigid class structure and mixing with the other staff and designers was not encouraged. Might give them ideas, don't you know," she smirked.

"Do you see any problem if I approach the two partners and invite them to lunch?"

She shook her head. "None that I can think of. I think it's a hell of a good idea. I'd like to do some of those same things in accounting and procurement too. We're supposed to be all one team but we haven't been operating that way. If you can crack that open I'm all for it."

"Well, that's an objective that isn't exactly in my job description," I said, "but it's something I'd like to do if I can."

"And I'd be happy to help any way I can," she smiled.

"Thanks, Janice, I appreciate that."

I left a voice mail message with Rueben and Dick inviting them to lunch on Thursday, my treat. I let them know I wanted to discuss the improvements in my department and "other issues." I was happy to get a single response from Dick Zarek saying they both would be pleased to accept my invitation. Mission accomplished.

Both men came to my office just before noon on Thursday. After a couple minutes small talk, we left for the elevators and lunch.

I chose a middle range restaurant not far from the office and both men indicated that they had eaten there a few times and it was good. I cheated and ordered a glass of wine, something I almost never did at lunch. My guests followed my lead. I wanted this to be informal and comfortable for all of us. It turned out just the way I'd hoped.

We had just finished our lunches when Rueben spoke up.

"You know, Dex, I think this is the first time anyone has ever made an attempt at desegregating the departments. About damn time too," he said forcefully.

"I agree," Dick added. "Your side of the business has been getting the short end of the stick for a while now and it has affected us. What you plan to do with design is really way overdue but to get us involved with your people is just as important."

"I'm surprised you've gotten along as well as you have with so little contact," I said.

"Oh ... we've had contact all right but it's been all one-sided. Us giving the design people what we want and then waiting for it. A lot of our younger engineers would benefit from being closer to the design people. Less likely to come up with underdeveloped work."

When we walked back to our office, I felt we had really set the groundwork for an improved relationship with the engineering group. Desegregation, Rueben called it. Pretty heavy word, I thought.

Chapter 7
A Different Kind of Progress

By week five, I had settled in and established the working model I wanted in the design department. As the new equipment arrived and the programs were either upgraded or replaced, I could see the attitude of the people really begin to shine. On top of that, Rueben and Dick had encouraged the other engineers to get involved with the designers and see what the new software could produce.

I implemented step-by-step training on the new stuff, with Terry being first, then Petra, then having the two of them help me bring the rest of the staff up to speed. I was pleased that the group as a whole was both cooperative and quick to pick up on the new materials. It was another step in our progress.

~~***~~

When I arrived in Toronto it had been the last week of winter and it felt like it. Cold, blustery winds off Lake Ontario combined with rain squalls made those first few days very unpleasant. Fortunately, I had plenty to occupy my time and if the weather was too grisly I could spend some hours in the various facilities at Rossmoor.

Now it was mid-April, and the baseball Blue Jays were back in town. Their home opener against the White Sox had already passed and with the improving weather and the retractable roof on the stadium there wouldn't be any rainouts. It would be something to do on the weekends, at least.

I spent some of my free time at the major attractions like the Royal Ontario Museum and the Art Gallery of Ontario. They were all within walking distance of my apartment. But by the end of April I was beginning to run out of new things to do. I hadn't bothered to rent a car yet. As long as I didn't need to go out of the Metro Toronto area, there were streetcars, buses, subway lines, and commuter trains to take me wherever I needed to go.

The twins had spoiled me for living on my own. In fact, they'd spoiled me for a lot of things including great meals, unlimited sex, companionship and just plain conversation. I'd been keeping in touch with them via Skype and it was good to see they were happy being home in Holland once more. I told them about my new job and some of the trials and tribulations I had encountered. I also told them about the end of my marriage.

There wasn't any likelihood that the twins and I would get back together again. The eighteen months we spent together was something unique and probably not repeatable. I didn't want to damage the memories I took from our time together. Better to leave them just as they were; delightful memories.

I had also been staying in touch with Jon and Merry. Again, Skype was great for Jon in Chile since it worked anytime he was near a high-speed Internet connection. I had signed on for a comprehensive cell phone plan so I called Merry on her cell. I had neglected my son and daughter when I was in the Caribbean and I wasn't going to do that again.

I didn't socialize with anyone in the Trent office, but I had been invited to a couple of barbeques in May and June and I decided that would be a nice diversion. Janice and I had become quite friendly as we were plotting the subversion of the rigid regime once dominant at Trent. In fact, when I thought about it, other than John Flannery, I had a good relationship with all of the staff regardless of department.

It was ironic that as I was thinking about Mr. Flannery and his hostility when I got a phone call from an unexpected source.

"Mr. McLeod, my name is Michelle Gauthier. I am a shareholder in Trent Engineering."

"Yes, Mrs. Gauthier, I know who you are. How can I help you?"

"I wonder if we could get together for lunch one day this week. I want to get to know the new people in the company and since you are a resident now, I thought I'd begin with you."

"I'd be happy to, Mrs. Gauthier. When would be convenient for you?"

"Would Thursday be all right?" she asked tentatively.

"Thursday will be fine. Where should we meet?"

"My late husband belonged to the University Club and I've retained his membership. Why don't we meet there? Oh by the way, you'll need to wear a tie. Sorry about that."

"That won't be a problem. Thursday noon at the University Club. I'll see you then," I said.

I wondered what this was about. I looked up the University Club website and saw immediately that I was being invited to a very posh setting. When I saw the lay of the land on my first day at Trent, I immediately took to wearing a suit and tie to work but more often than not I discarded the jacket and loosened the tie when I arrived in my office. As far as John Flannery knew, I conformed to the dress code throughout the day.

It was a short distance to the club via streetcar and I left the office in plenty of time to make the noon appointment. I arrived a few minutes early, announced myself to the maitre d' and was immediately seated at a very nice table along the wall. I was barely in the chair when an attractive forty-something woman approached and smiled.

"You must be Dexter McLeod," she said brightly. "I'm Michelle Gauthier."

I rose and took her hand. "Very nice to meet you, Mrs. Gauthier."

"Oh please, it's Michelle. I understand you go by Dex. Is that correct?"

"Yes, I'm afraid it is."

"Don't be embarrassed, Dex. From what I hear, you're single-handedly changing the culture at Trent, and for the better I might add."

"I plead guilty with extenuating circumstances, ma'am."

She laughed with genuine humour.

"I'm told you weren't exactly welcomed with open arms by John Flannery. No surprise there," she said, still with a smile.

"No … he wasn't pleased to see 'some upstart from the west' invade his kingdom."

Again she laughed. "Ah, Janice was right, you are a breath of fresh air."

"Oh … so that's where you're getting your inside information," I said with a grin.

"Yes … her and other places. You've made quite an impression in a very short time. I had to meet you to find out just who John Flannery's nemesis was."

"Well, I'm not trying to be his nemesis. My main objective is to stay out of his way. So far, so good."

We decided to look at the menus and a few minutes later after I filled her in on my background, the waiter arrived and we ordered.

"What do you think will happen with John, Michelle?" We had comfortably progressed to a first name basis.

"I'll tell you something you probably don't know. John hasn't always been the curmudgeon he is today. Five years ago, his wife was diagnosed with Multiple Sclerosis. Katherine and John have been together since college, over forty years. They remain deeply in love and committed to each other.

"While that was going on, two of the senior partners retired and then my husband, David, died suddenly. It left the company stripped of the energy and vitality that made it go. You add those two stresses to a man like John and it isn't hard to imagine how he could be pushed to the breaking point."

"I had heard that his wife was ill but your knowledge of him makes his behaviour almost understandable. Why doesn't he retire?" I asked.

"Trent is all he has to occupy his time. He's devoted to Katherine so he comes in to the office to give both of them a break, then leaves early to be home with her as soon as possible."

"He'd be better off taking a leave of absence and taking his wife on a long trip or a cruise while he still can. At least they'd be able to spend more of their time together while she's still able to enjoy it."

Michelle looked at me as if she was seeing me for the first time.

"Why didn't I think of that?" she said quietly. "Rueben tells me he hasn't anything to do at the office. He just sits there and reads the newspaper or the financial reports. He doesn't see anyone. Has he even come into your department?"

"No. Not while I've been there."

She sat back in her chair, looking intently at me but her thoughts were on something else entirely.

"When you go back to the office this afternoon, I'm coming along. I think it's time I had a chat with Mr. John Flannery."

She didn't present her comment with any thought that I'd object so I nodded. Perhaps she could bring him out of his shell. Both of them were hurting; Michelle from the loss of her husband and John from his wife's illness. It couldn't do any harm, I thought.

Michelle signed the bill and I thanked her for the excellent lunch. It was an unexpected pleasure. As we walked out of the dining room, I surveyed the attractive widow. Five-foot-five or six, I guessed, attractive mature build, carefully coiffed silver-blonde hair, nice ass, and a confident stride. All-in-all, a very lovely package.

"How did you get here, Dex?" she asked as we exited the building.

"Oh … I took the streetcar."

"Excellent, so did I. Let's go."

Well, how about that. No Mercedes or even a taxi. This lady was happy with the public transit. Just another point in her favour.

"Where are you staying, Dex?"

"At the Rossmoor Suites. Only a block or so from the office."

"Yes. Good choice. I think Tom Yardley and Wolf stayed there when we were discussing the merger."

"I have a question you may not want to answer," I said carefully.

"Go ahead," she said, curiosity written on her expression.

"Were you happy with the acquisition/merger?"

"Yes," she answered unhesitatingly. "I knew it was necessary and so did Reuben and Dick. I was impressed with Tom and Wolf. Particularly Wolf. He is a German version of my late husband. Lots of confidence and lots of energy. He'll make a big difference to Trent if I'm any judge of character."

"That's his track record at Pinecone, and I don't see any reason it won't continue here. I'm glad you approve, though. I'm sure Tom and Wolf want the other partners to be happy with the new company. As far as I can tell, Reuben and Dick are."

"Absolutely! But then, I think you have been a big factor in that. All I hear from my sources is that Dexter McLeod is a really nice guy. The smartest moves you made right in the beginning were to fix up the lunch room and form the committees to get the work done. No one had ever done anything like that before."

"Simple stuff, really. If you give people a good place to work they'll do better."

"Sometimes the simple stuff isn't so simple," she said with a wry grin. "Anyway, my congratulations on your success so far. Now, let's see if I can help with John Flannery," she said as we stepped down from the streetcar.

We walked to the office building and entered the elevator, rising quickly in the nearly empty car. I held the door for her into the office and we walked to Brigit's reception desk.

"Hi, Mrs. Gauthier," Brigit said enthusiastically. "How nice to see you again." Brigit was looking curiously at both Michelle and me, wondering I suppose what we were doing together.

"Nice to see you too, Brigit. Would you tell John I'd like to see him, please? I'm sure he's not busy," she said with raised eyebrows and a grin.

"Thank you again for lunch, Mich … Mrs. Gauthier," I stumbled. "I hope I can reciprocate some time in the future."

"My pleasure entirely, Dexter. Thank you for joining me. I know we will be in touch," she said with another of her lovely, genuine smiles.

I could see Brigit's eyes flicking back and forth as we parted. She was fascinated by this turn of events. I may have created another of the mysteries about who I really was. I was pretty sure I had a good portion of the staff baffled. I just kept doing things they didn't expect. Not bad things, mind you, just different.

I was humming to myself as I walked back to my office. A very fine lunch with an attractive widow can do that for you. She might be way out of my league but it was nice to have the opportunity to spend some time with her.

I went back to work and got back to updating my report for Tom. I had been sending him progress reports weekly and, although he hadn't asked for them that frequently, I was happy to provide them. It was a way for me to remember what had gone on in the previous five days and Tom commented that he enjoyed hearing some of the office gossip and reaction to my presence along with the dry facts of our progress toward bringing the department up to Vancouver standards.

Just before quitting time at five o'clock, Janice walked into my office, closed the door behind her, plunked herself down in the closest chair and said, "Okay, Dex, give! What's with you and Michelle having lunch?"

I chuckled as she gave me the "no nonsense" stare. She had a hard time pulling it off, mainly because her curiosity got the better of her.

"Whatever do you mean, Janice?" I asked, feigning ignorance.

"Don't give me that! When our most eligible bachelor has lunch with our most eligible widow, something is going on," she said emphatically.

"Well, it wasn't my idea. Michelle just wanted to meet me. Besides, you've been feeding her information all along so you shouldn't be surprised," I said, hoping to knock her off stride.

It must have worked. She looked taken aback and sat silent for a moment before responding.

"She's a great lady, Dex. And you've probably noticed she very attractive too," Janice said more carefully.

"Janice, she's way out of my league. Besides, I think you're adding two and two and coming up with six or seven."

"I noticed you were on a first name basis," she accused.

"Her idea. I always bow to the wishes of the partners," I grinned.

"Pardon my language, but that's horsebuns."

"Naughty, naughty, Janice. That kind of language doesn't fit the Flannery code of conduct."

Janice sighed, showed me a rueful smile, and shook her head.

"Look, Dex, there are a half-dozen single women in this office that would kill for a date with you and a few married ones as well. The day you showed up in this office you had their undivided attention. Now you come prancing back from lunch with Michelle Gauthier on your arm. So don't try and tell me nothing's going on."

Janice and I had obviously progressed passed the informal familiarity stage right to blunt comment. Still, I couldn't be upset with her. She was the matriarch of the female staff and a valuable confidant in matters involving the office personnel and the company's history. She was in her mid-fifties and had been with Trent for over twenty years.

"That's a pretty big leap, Janice. One lunch and I'm the widow's new man?"

"You will be if she has anything to do with it. Michelle and I go way back. I'll get the scoop on your lunch before you know it. Then I'll have a better handle on the situation," she said with a smirk.

I was shaking my head. "Aren't there any other single eligible men in this office?"

"None that are attractive vice presidents who are smoother than a baby's bottom when it comes to handling people. You may just be at the right place at the right time, Dex. Don't fight it. Go with the flow," she chuckled, rising from her chair and heading for the door. "I'll see you in the morning," she said with another of those sly smiles I'd come to recognize.

As Janice left, Brigit came back to my office and handed me a card.

"Mrs. Gauthier asked me to give this to you," she smiled knowingly.

Damn, is everyone in on some kind of conspiracy here? I looked at the card. *Michelle Gauthier, Suite 2101, Lakeside Place, Toronto, ON.* It also had a phone number, but nothing else. Interesting.

I got an unexpected call from Tom Yardley late Friday morning. After the usual pleasantries he got down to business.

"How are you coming on the project?"

"Good, Tom. I think we're ahead of where I expected to be. I'm getting great cooperation here I'm happy to say."

"Good for you, Dex. I knew you'd come through. Do you think you can spare a bit of time for a side project?"

"What have you got in mind?"

"Our accounting people want to be able to talk to Trent's system, but right now we're on two different packages. We'd like to replace what they've got with our program. Can you help with that?"

"Sure. I don't know anything about accounting, though."

"Not a problem. We'll send Pete Thorpe down to do the setup and training. He shouldn't take more than a week."

"Sure, good choice. Why don't you have Pete stay with me? I've got a spare bedroom and it'll save some money."

"If you're okay with that then that's what we'll do. We'll courier out the software tonight so you should have it Monday. I'll talk to Pete and see when he can go."

"Fine ... no problem. I wouldn't mind some company for a few days."

"Getting lonely down there?" Tom chuckled. "No twins to keep you occupied?"

"Nope, not yet. But ... I keep hoping."

After I hung up, I wondered just what I was going to do about finding some companionship. To be fair, I hadn't really tried very hard. Maybe with Pete around we could go hunting together. He was a confirmed bachelor and had a reputation for seldom being without a woman. In the meantime, he was still in Vancouver and I was looking at another open weekend in Toronto.

That evening I decided to have a light supper at a local pub only a few minutes walk from my apartment. I'd had lunch there a few times on the weekend and found the food quite acceptable. It was a large sports bar with plenty of Maple Leaf, Raptors, Argos and Blue Jays memorabilia, along with a half-dozen flat screen TVs. If nothing else I could sit there and watch the baseball game.

By the time I'd changed my clothes, washed up and headed out the door, it was almost seven o'clock. It was a reasonably mild spring evening and the walk to the pub was quite pleasant. The place was busy so I took a seat at the bar and ordered a draft beer. Looking around, the crowd was quite young, many of them business people having a Friday after-work drink before heading home I guessed. Looking at all the youthful faces, I began to feel quite old. I was forty-seven, almost fifty … half a century. Single and no female prospects. Bloody depressing.

I'd finished my steak sandwich and had just ordered my second beer when I was conscious of a new body occupying the seat to my right. What attracted my attention was the scent of perfume. I turned to look at her and got a pleasant surprise. She was mid-thirties by appearances and quite good-looking.

"Evening," I said quietly.

"Hi," she responded.

Not much in the way of a conversation so far. I decided to let it be. If she wanted to talk to me she would.

She'd ordered some kind of cocktail that I couldn't identify. I checked out her clothing and decided she wasn't a business person. The dress was definitely not for office wear. A short skirt, a tight-fitting top, a fair amount of jewellery and an excess of makeup. She was attractive but a little too over-the-top for my tastes.

"You done looking?" she asked without a smile.

"Pretty much," I said, scrambling not to look and sound like a jerk. "Sorry if it bothered you."

She didn't reply but looked straight ahead. After an awkward silence, she opened her purse and took out a cell phone. She punched in a speed dial code and waited.

"Where are you," she said in a not too subtle tone.

A pause.

"Oh great! I get dressed up to come down here for you and now you can't make it. Thanks a lot."

Another pause.

"Forget it. You're totally unreliable, Tony. Go take your mama some chicken soup and kiss her good night. It's the only action you're going to get."

She snapped the phone shut, mumbling something about goddamned momma's boy. She was steaming but trying to keep it under control. She turned to me and began to vent.

"Can you imagine a forty-year-old guy who can't do anything without checking with his mother?"

I turned and realized she was talking to me.

"Yup. See it all the time on situation comedies. Not so much in real life, though."

"Wise guy," she said, then began to laugh. Not loud or hearty but more a low, rumbling chuckle, all the while shaking her head.

"Honest to God, I don't know if I'll ever find a guy who can stand on his own two feet, make an honest living and treat me like he actually cares," she said sourly.

"You're pretty young to be panicking, aren't you?" I asked.

"Not that young, mister. The other side of thirty is usually panic time for single women."

"Well, if it cheers you up any, I'm almost fifty and single so it can't be all that bad."

"Look at me, pal. I'm dressed like a slut so I can get a rise out of the jerk I'm trying to tie down and it's all for nothing. I'm afraid to smile in case my makeup cracks."

I started to laugh. She was making fun of herself and when I laughed, she broke down and did too.

"It isn't funny," she finally managed. "I've made enough bad choices in men to last a lifetime. One of these days, the law of averages says I'm going to hit it lucky."

"If you date enough guys, sooner or later you'll find someone. You're an attractive woman when you want to be. You've got a sense of humour."

"What do you mean 'when I want to be?'"

"Well, maybe a little less makeup and a little less skin might be in order."

"What are you, some kind of fashion critic?" she demanded.

"Nope. Just observing what makes guys like me attracted to women like you."

There was another silence as she sipped her drink. It was a minute or so later that she spoke again.

"Save my seat for me will you?" she said, picking up her purse and heading for the ladies room.

"Sure. You want another drink?"

She stopped and looked at me and made a decision. "Please."

I signaled the bartender.

"What's she drinking?"

"Can you believe it, a Shirley Temple?" He looked bewildered at her choice.

So, another surprise. "Maybe the lady doesn't drink?"

She arrived back at her seat five minutes later and I did a classic double take when she did. Gone was the makeup, replaced with just lipstick. The dress somehow or other had lengthened at least three inches, and the top was now much less revealing. The transformation was amazing.

"What the hell did you do to yourself," I asked.

"Why, do I look worse?"

"Hell, no. You look great. Very sexy. No sign of slutty. Very nice," I said sincerely.

"Thanks. Just a little trick I learned many years ago. It would have been wasted on Tony so I thought I'd see what Mr. Critic thought of it."

"Mr. Critic, Dex by name, thinks you did yourself a big favour."

"Glad you like it. I'm Rose … Rosalind Tulloch, actually," said, extending her hand. I took it gently and shook it.

"Nice to meet you, Rose."

There was another pause in the conversation until I asked, "What were you and Tony going to do this evening?"

"He was supposed to take me dancing. There's a club just up the street that has a nice band and the cover isn't too bad. I was really looking forward to it."

"What kind of music?" I asked.

"Middle of the road, stuff. I don't go for these disco places. Too loud and too impersonal."

I nodded. "I know what you mean. But it's a little early isn't it?"

She looked at her watch. "Not too early. They start at nine so if you want a decent table you don't want to show up at ten."

I looked at my watch. It was just coming up to nine pm. I thought what the hell. What could she say but yes or no.

"Well, I'd be happy to take you dancing if you can stand hanging out with an old geezer like me."

She looked at me with a curious expression, then gave me a thorough once over.

"You don't look that old. You dress nice and you are polite. Maybe I can take a chance if you promise to behave," she said.

"Oh ... behave. Well, you better tell me what is out of bounds then," I kidded.

She socked me on the arm. "You know damn well what I mean. I'm going to have to fight you off all night?"

"Absolutely. They don't call me the octopus for nothing."

She looked at me long and hard once more.

"I don't believe you. So ... I guess I'll take a chance that you are okay."

"Great, let's go. Since I'm not from around here I'll let you lead the way."

"Where are you from?" she asked as she slipped off the stool.

"Vancouver. I'm here on a business assignment."

"Figures," she said sourly. "Just when I meet an interesting guy, he's from out of town. Come on, Dex. Let's get this show on the road. My feet are getting itchy."

We walked briskly up the street and around the corner. I suppose we walked three blocks before we came to the well-lit entrance of the *York Palladium*. It looked like it might have been a theatre at one time but the posters were advertising an upcoming ballroom dance contest.

"Say, am I going to be all right without a tie?" I asked her. I was wearing a polo shirt, a blue blazer, slacks and loafers.

"Yeah, you look fine. You should see some of the outfits people wear to this place."

I paid the cover and we proceeded into the ballroom. It was big, fairly well lit without being bright, and not yet too crowded or noisy. A band was on the stage playing some seventies standards and the music was quite good.

"I hope you're not expecting Fred Astaire," I said as we found a table.

"I have a feeling you'll be fine, Dex," she said with a smile.

There was no point in sitting, since neither of us wanted a drink, so I offered her my hand and led her to the dance floor. It was a medium-slow number, just right to get the feel of how we were going to fit together. I shouldn't have worried.

Rose was light on her feet and we seemed to be in synch with each other right from the start. I could feel her relax halfway through the first number and when she did, I did too. It was the start of a very pleasant evening.

"I'm really glad I suggested this," I told her after our first few dances. "You are very easy to dance with and I'm really enjoying myself.

"Thank you, Dex," Rose said with a nice, warm smile. "I'm having a good time too. You and I seem to dance pretty well together."

"We do, don't we. Can I get you something to drink?"

"Just a soft drink … maybe a Coke, please."

"Coming right up," I said heading for the bar.

When I got back to our table, a couple of guys were talking to Rose and the look on her face told me she wasn't too comfortable.

"Evening, gentlemen," I said politely as I put the drinks down on the table. "Something I can help you with?"

They looked at me, then each other, shook their heads and left.

"I hope they didn't upset you, Rose."

"No, just trying their luck. That's pretty typical of what happens when women are sitting alone in these places. But thanks for asking," she said with a nice smile.

The evening seemed to whiz by very quickly and soon it was time to leave. As we walked out onto the street, I asked Rose, "Where do you live? How will you get home?"

"Oh, I live in Scarborough. I'll take the subway and catch a bus from there," she said.

"No. I don't think that's a good idea at this time of night. You've trusted me this far, trust me to get you home safely," I said, turning to hail a cab.

She put up some resistance but in the end I persuaded her to let me get her home quickly and safely. I didn't have any ulterior motive. She had been a cheap date, a non-drinker, and I was feeling good about how much I enjoyed her company and the dancing.

"Where are you living, Dex?" she asked as the cab moved quickly up the Don Mills Parkway.

"I'm in a suites hotel downtown, the Rossmoor. It's only a block from our office."

"Are you going to be here for a while?"

"Yes. I'm involved in a project to modernize our design department. I could be here for several months if things get complicated."

"Well, if you're looking for a date sometime, call me," she said with a smile. She took a notepad and pen out of her purse, wrote a phone number on it, ripped it out and handed it to me. "You were a perfect gentleman and I had a really good time. If you're wondering, I'd go out with you anytime."

"Thank you, Rose. That's very nice of you to say so. I may just do that," I said, reaching in my blazer vest pocket and pulling out my business card. I borrowed her pen and wrote the Rossmoor phone number on the back, since my cards showed my Vancouver address.

The taxi pulled up in front of an apartment block, and Rose began to get out. I told the driver to wait and I walked around to the sidewalk side and helped Rose with the door. I walked her the short distance to the lobby door and stopped. She turned to me, smiled and kissed me lightly on the lips.

"Thank you again, Dexter McLeod. That was a very nice evening. I meant what I said about being happy to go out with again. Don't forget me now."

"I won't. I promise. Thank you for taking a chance on me and letting me have a great evening as well. Good night."

I watched her step into the lobby and push the button for the elevator. I waved and she waved back as she moved into the car and the doors closed. I returned to the cab and gave the driver the Rossmoor address. As we began to retrace our path, I thought what a pleasant young woman Rose was. It was difficult to understand why she didn't have a number of guys interested in her.

Chapter 8
A Surplus of Opportunities

When I let myself into the office on Monday morning, I noticed I wasn't the first one to arrive. After flicking on the lights in the design department, I took a stroll around the office to see who was here. It was Janice and she was busy with something on her computer.

"Good morning, Dex," she said without looking up. "Grab me a coffee will you; cream and sugar please. It should be ready by now."

"On my way," I said, wondering what was going on.

The lights were on in the lunch room and the two-pot coffee maker was sitting with both sides full. After pouring two mugs, I headed back to Janice's area and put one down, drawing up a chair for myself.

"What's going on? This is pretty early for you. Do we have a problem?"

"No … not really," she said, stopping her typing and turning toward me.

"Michelle phoned me last night. John Flannery has decided to take an indefinite leave of absence. He and Katherine are going on an around the world trip. Michelle tells me it was all your idea," she smiled lightly.

"Well, isn't that something. I did suggest it to Michelle but I didn't think he'd go for it. But, I suppose that is a good sign."

"Michelle can be very persuasive when she needs to be. But really, you came up with a very good idea and John can go without having to sacrifice his position at Trent. Very well thought out, Dex."

"Thanks for the compliment but it was just a spur-of-the-moment suggestion."

Janice shrugged.

"I guess that begs the question, who will the interim president be?" I asked.

"I think Michelle, Rueben, and Dick are going to have a conference call with Tom Yardley and Wolf. We'll let them thrash it out," she grinned.

"Well, I hope this helps Flannery and his wife. He's a pretty unhappy man right now and he's not able to contribute the way he probably wants to. Good luck to him," I said.

"Yes ... good luck to him," she said quietly. "I'm just tidying up the details of his financial arrangements. He'll still be on the company health insurance and benefits but his salary will be suspended."

"Will they be all right ... financially, I mean."

"Oh yeah ... he's very well off and I think his wife is as well. She's old Toronto money. They're fine."

"Well ... that's one way to start the week, I guess," I said. I didn't feel particularly good at that moment and I guess it showed.

"Hey, Dex. This wasn't really your doing. You just planted the seed in Michelle's mind. Besides, I think you know that this is the best thing for both of them."

"I know, Janice. I just wish we'd got along better at the start. I feel like I've been going behind his back and doing things he wouldn't approve of. I don't feel good about that."

"You think he didn't know what was going on?" she snorted. "John knew ... and saw ... what you were doing. At first he didn't like it but as things began to take shape he could see what was happening. He told me that he knew it was overdue. He just wished he could have been part of it."

"When is he leaving? I'd like to say goodbye to him and wish him well," I said, wondering if I really meant it.

"He's already left, Dex. He won't be back any time soon, if at all," she said sadly.

We sat quietly, sipping our coffees and thinking our private thoughts. I felt badly that John Flannery had been so upset with the merger and with my showing up ready to change things. I was only glad that I hadn't forced a confrontation with him. That would have made things worse. I worked around him and with luck and a lot of cooperation from the people, we got things done.

I walked back to my office, leaving Janice to finish up whatever she was doing. I sat in my office staring at my monitor, but doing nothing for a few minutes. Finally, I pulled myself out of the funk I was in and got back to work. Whatever the reasons, John Flannery was gone and there would be a new leader at Trent Engineering in the next day or so.

By 8:30 that morning, the word was out. A notice had been placed on the bulletin board in the lunch room and an e-mail circulated to all the staff at Trent. I assumed Tom would look after notifying the Pinecone staff.

I expected to hear from Tom by ten o'clock that morning and he didn't disappoint me.

"Morning, Dex. I know you've heard the news, so I won't dwell on it. Michelle Gauthier called me on the weekend to tell me about her meeting with John and his decision. She says it was your suggestion that led to her proposing it to him. Once again you prove just how valuable you are to this organization. Well done and nicely handled too."

"I hope it's the right solution for them," I said. "I don't feel great about it but if it helps him and his wife, then I can live with it."

"It's a perfect solution, Dex. It allows him to keep his pride and his status but also gives him a chance to be with his wife for however long he can care for her."

"Have you decided on who will take over for him … temporarily?" I asked, desperate to change the topic.

"Rueben Golowitz will be nominated by Michelle, seconded by me. I don't think it will cause any stir. He's the senior man now so it's a logical choice. Michelle has already covered it off with Zarek and he's fine with it."

"Good. I think that's a good choice too. He and Dick have been very supportive of what we've been doing so we can carry on without interruption."

"I meant what I said, Dex. You really have a knack for getting people on your side. It makes you a very valuable resource for us. Maybe you missed your calling. Perhaps you should have been a diplomat," he chuckled.

"Nice of you to say so, Tom, but I like what I do, I'm happy where I am and I'm being very well rewarded by you. I have no complaints."

"Good to hear it, Dex. I know I can call on you when something like this comes up. If you need anything at all, I'm only a phone call away."

"Thanks, Tom. I really do appreciate it … and thank Wolf too when you see him."

I hung up the phone feeling pretty damn good. I hadn't really paid any attention to my salary since I was appointed vice president until I saw the first semi-monthly deposit in my account. I was certainly being paid like a vice president so I had to accept that I was confirmed in the role.

Pete Thorpe showed up early Wednesday evening, arriving from the airport by cab. He greeted me enthusiastically, looking around and clearly approving of our accommodations.

"Jeez, Dex, this is great. This is better than my place back home."

"It should be, Pete. It's renting for three grand a month, and that's a special for us."

"I don't know, Dex. Downtown Toronto, right in the heart of action central. Couldn't get much better than this," he enthused.

"You aren't going to be here that long, Pete. How about we agree no one-night-stands here."

"Ouch, that does limit my options ... but ... it's your place and you're the vice president, so your rules count."

"Good. Now ... have you eaten yet?"

"No ... they cleverly scheduled the flight to avoid serving one of their gourmet meals," he smirked.

"Fine. Let's go down the street to my local pub. The food's good and it should be quiet tonight."

Pete gave me a quick approval and we set out for our evening meal.

There weren't that many people in the place when we arrived. The Blue Jays were out of town and the Maple Leafs had finished another dismal season, missing the playoffs for the umpteenth time.

"If you're a good boy I'll treat you to a game next week. The Red Sox are in town."

"What's your definition of a good boy?"

"Oh, let's say the staff training is on or ahead of schedule and you behave yourself after hours," I grinned.

"You drive a hard bargain, Mr. Vice President. But … for the Red Sox, I'm going to be very diligent in my work."

"I would expect nothing less from you, Pete."

And I wouldn't, either. Pete may have been a persistent womanizer but he was good at his job and didn't mix business with pleasure. He may not have been my ideal roommate, but for a week or so I could handle it.

Pete did his job in his usual workmanlike fashion and when he left I was confident the Trent accounting staff had what they needed to blend in with the Vancouver standard accounting system. The Red Sox had beaten the Jays 2-0 the night before he left but he was pleased to have seen the game from one of the skyboxes. A generous hardware supplier had offered a couple of seats in their private box and I think Pete was pretty impressed.

As we entered May, I began to get a feel for just how long my presence would be needed in Toronto. The training on the new equipment and software was going well and I thought before the end of July I would be able to return to my hometown with confidence that Terry and Petra could handle the growth in the future. I was always available for emergencies so I wasn't too worried that I would be leaving too soon.

We had already begun to feel the effects of Wolf's efforts at finding some new opportunities. Plus, Vancouver was very busy and wanted to hive off some work to Toronto, knowing it would be handled properly with me there. I sat down with Terry, Petra and Rueben and discussed adding two more people.

When we went over the current and future work, more staff appeared to be necessary. It would put an extra training burden on me and my two senior people but this wasn't the time to turn down opportunities to grow. I also was mindful of the image that it would project inside the office. Positive things were happening again. Trent was hiring!

I had a routine when hiring new designers. I would interview them first to weed out the ones I thought were the weakest or otherwise not suitable. Then I would pass the "keepers" along to Terry and Petra to individually interview the remaining candidates. Then we would meet and discuss what we thought of each of them. It tended to give a more rounded picture of the candidates since we all had our own individual biases and interests.

In the end, we found two very good young men who all three of us agreed would be a good fit for our department. In fact, we could have chosen four or five of the candidates and not compromised our objectives. That was a good sign. As Trent continued to grow we would have some confidence that we could find new talent fairly promptly.

Victoria Day, or May Day as it was often called, fell on a Monday, and it was decided a family barbeque/picnic was in order. We chose to hold the event on the Sunday, giving both the adults and the children a chance to recover from the event and attend family or community outings on Monday as well.

We estimated that a hundred men, women and children would attend so we needed a location that could handle that many people. It was Dick Zarek that came up with the answer. His uncle owned a farm north of the city near Bolton and he could provide not only the space, but horses for riding and farm animals for the kids to visit.

I was a little concerned that it was a long way for some of the families so with Rueben's help, we hired two school busses to pick up anyone who wanted a ride. More than seventy people thought that was the way to go so we set up a simple bus route from the city to the farm. The first bus would leave at one o'clock in the afternoon and the second at two o'clock. It wasn't perfect but we got a lot of compliments for making the effort. The busses would leave the farm at eight and nine o'clock that evening to get everyone home at a reasonable hour.

I discovered that no one had done anything like this in quite a few years. Janice said the word around the office was that the people felt Trent was becoming a whole new company and they liked what they saw. That gave me some confidence that we were doing the right thing.

I asked for volunteers to help with the organization and had no problem getting more than we needed. I left it to Janice to suggest what games the kids would enjoy. She even suggested we rent an open canopy in case it rained or, if on the other hand, it got very warm. I thought that was a wise precaution. Since I was spending Trent's money, I talked all my decisions over with Rueben but he was in complete agreement. The whole day would cost less than $2500 and we viewed that as a good investment in morale.

I made sure I sent an invitation to Michelle as well. I doubted she would come but I wanted to make the gesture. Surprise, surprise, she accepted and chose to ride the bus to the farm. I thought about my own situation and decided to phone Rose Tulloch.

"Hi, Rose. This is Dexter McLeod. I don't know if you remember me."

"Of course I do, Dex. A girl doesn't forget her favorite dance partner that easily."

"Great. Say … our company is having a May Day weekend picnic at a farm up in Bolton on Sunday. I was wondering if you'd like to be my guest?"

"I'd love to. Thank you for thinking of me."

Her acceptance was enthusiastic and I was pleased about that. I made arrangements to pick her up at her apartment since I was renting a people van just in case we had some stragglers or we needed to make an emergency run to town. It cost very little more than a car so it was an easy decision.

When the chosen Sunday rolled around, it dawned sunny with a bit of scattered cloud. Almost perfect, I thought. I had arranged to pick Rose up just after two o'clock which would allow me to check out the bus situation and make sure no one got left behind. There must have been a lot of enthusiasm for this picnic because everyone was on time, if not early. I drove to Rose's apartment building and she was waiting for me as I drove up.

"I hope I didn't keep you waiting too long, Rose."

"No … besides, it's a lovely sunny day and I'm really looking forward to the picnic. I haven't been on one of these for years … not since I was a teenager."

We caught up on each other's activities over the past weeks and she confirmed that Tony had been dumped that night when we went dancing. She said she knew when she was out with me that she was settling for less and she didn't want to do that. I agreed with her decision.

We arrived at the farm and it was already a sea of activity. Kids running in every direction, a softball game getting underway, horseback rides getting organized and a petting zoo for the little ones. It was great to see everyone getting involved.

As we walked toward the canopy and the centre of activity, I spotted Michelle and led Rose toward her.

"Hi, Michelle, glad you could make it. I'd like you to meet Rose Tulloch. Rose, this is one of our partners, Michelle Gauthier."

"Nice to meet you, Rose," Michelle said, looking her over carefully.

We exchanged some small talk about the picnic and the weather before we moved off. It seemed like an awkward exchange and I wondered why. Rose answered that question for me.

"I think Michelle is a little upset that you're with me, Dex."

"What makes you say that?"

"Well, most women can tell when another woman has ideas about a guy. I think she is disappointed that you aren't with her. Did you let on that you would be her date?"

"No ... not at all. But ... I guess maybe she took it for granted that ... well ... since I asked her if she would like to attend. Oh shit!"

Rose laughed. "You are so screwed, Dex. For a vice president, you need some training in handling women. You must have done better than this in the past."

"You'd think so since I was married for over twenty years. I guess I forgot my manners somewhere along the way."

"Don't get too upset, Dex. It's fixable. Leave it to me."

"What's that mean?"

"Never mind ... just leave it to me," she laughed.

She seemed to be having fun at my expense. I was upset with myself for letting Michelle think I had invited her to be with me. We'd hardly got here and I'd already screwed up. Not a good start to the day.

We had decided that today would be a BYOB picnic. No alcohol would be supplied but if you wanted to bring your own, you were asked to use discretion and common sense. Several of us agreed to keep an eye on anyone who looked like they might be overindulging.

Rose had wandered off to see the sights and I was sitting on a fence rail watching the young people having fun riding the three horses Dick's uncle had saddled. I wasn't really paying attention and when I felt a hand on my arm I jumped in surprise.

"Sorry, Dex," Michelle apologized. "I saw you here by yourself and thought I'd come by and keep you company. What happened to Rose?"

"Uhhm, she's gone off to see what's going on. She's pretty independent I guess."

"Have you known her long?"

"No … in fact we've only been out once back in April. Look Michelle, please let me apologize for being …." I didn't get any further as she put her finger to my lips.

"Don't. I'm not offended. I think I know enough about you that you didn't expect me to be your date."

"To be honest, Michelle, the thought didn't even cross my mind," I said, immediately regretting it.

"Oh … now I am offended," she said with a sneaky grin. "Don't you think I'm date material?"

"No ... no ... I mean yes you are definitely date material but I never thought ... I mean ... we don't exactly run in the same circles."

She was laughing lightly now and I was sure my face looked like I'd acquired an instant sunburn.

"You keep underestimating yourself, Dexter McLeod. What woman wouldn't be attracted to a man with your special talents? I don't think I've ever met anyone who is so universally liked. Surely you can get your back up now and then, can't you?"

"Yes I can, as my ex-wife found out some time ago. There are times when I don't back down. I work hard to avoid confrontation when it isn't necessary but I don't run from it. I hope that doesn't sound too strident," I said, again tinged with apology.

"No, not at all. That's good to know. I'll keep it in mind," she said thoughtfully. "In the meantime, would you like to join me at the theatre next weekend? I have two tickets to '*I'm All Right, Jack,*' a good old-fashioned comedy."

"I'd love to. I haven't been to the theatre in a long time. I know the plot so I'll undoubtedly compare the actors to Peter Sellers and Ian Carmichael. Thank you very much for inviting me," I smiled.

"We'll have dinner as well. The performance starts at eight. Would you prefer to eat before or after?"

"Well, to be honest, I prefer before if that's all right with you."

"I prefer to eat before as well. Those late night meals take too long to digest. I'll make the reservations on line tomorrow. It should be good fun," she said happily.

We spent some time with small talk about the picnic and how people were getting along at the office. Michelle seemed very interested in the progress we were making. She had never worked at the office but had been keenly interested in her husband's work and the people he worked with. I could understand why she would use Janice as a conduit of information. Both of them were discreet but inquisitive by nature.

I saw Rose approaching, happily walking along with a soft drink in her hand.

"Can I take my escort back now, Michelle?" she kidded.

"Yes ... he's all yours, Rose. Quite a nice fellow, too."

They were having some fun at my expense, obviously having conspired in some way to get me alone with Michelle.

We walked toward the canopy and the food serving area.

"Well, did I give you enough time?" Rose asked merrily.

"Enough time for what?"

"For one of you to ask the other for a date. Jeez, Dex. I thought that was obvious."

"I had no intention of asking Michelle for a date when I was already here with you. That would be rude."

"Oh, come on, Dex. You're not here in Toronto for that much longer and I'm going to be around after you've gone. So ... I took the opportunity to scout out the territory with a little help from Michelle and Janice."

"How do you know Janice?"

"I didn't until Michelle introduced us. She's a fountain of knowledge. I've already met one very nice eligible bachelor and I've only just gotten started," she boasted.

"Did you plan this all along, Rose? I mean, before we got here you had never met Michelle or Janice. Now all of a sudden you are on a first name basis."

"Well Dex, it seems that you are infatuated with Michelle and she's fascinated with you. That much is obvious and Janice confirmed it. So, since I'm not going to be in the picture, I thought I'd do a little scouting while I had the chance. I met a very nice English gentleman who seemed to be quite interested in me."

"You must mean, Miles Wilder."

"Yup. It's nice to meet a gentleman with manners as good as yours, Dex. It isn't that common these days."

"Miles is a good guy and is doing very well at our office. He would be good boyfriend material I think."

"Now who's trying to set who up?" she chortled.

We walked for a few moments before Rose spoke.

"Are you upset that I kind of abandoned you and went looking?"

"No ... not really. I mean, I did ask you to come with me so I should be a little put off but ... you're right. I'm not going to be here forever so I can't blame you for taking advantage of the situation. Just about any single guy here would be better than Tony," I laughed.

"Oh so true. So look, Dex. Since Michelle is all alone and Miles didn't bring a date to the picnic, would you be upset if I looked after Miles and you looked after Michelle?"

"No, I guess not. But if it doesn't work out with Miles, you know where to find me if you want to go dancing some Friday night."

"You've got a deal. But you know what, Dex, in a way I hope I don't have to call you. I hope you aren't offended by that."

"Not … I know what you mean. Good luck and let me know when you want to go home."

"Thanks, Dex," she said, giving me a quick kiss on the cheek.

I turned back to the corral and saw Michelle watching us. As Rose skipped away, I made a decision and walked back up the slope to where she was standing.

"Well, that was a short romance," she laughed as I approached.

"It was never intended to be a romance. Just friends. Now she's discovered the charms of another man, so I'm history."

"She really thinks a lot of you, Dex. Just like most of the other women who know you. But she's a realist. She wants a stay-at-home man and in her mind that's not you. You'll be back in Vancouver and she'll still be here."

"I'm too old for her anyway, Michelle. Fifteen years is a big gap."

"Not if it's the right guy. If you were a local, she'd be giving you the full-court-press I think she called it. But she's not upset or discouraged. I think when she dumped her old boyfriend and went dancing with you she realized there were other nice men in the world. I hope she finds one."

"Me too. She is a nice woman. You never know who you're going to meet in a pub or at a picnic," I grinned.

"Or at the University Club," she said slyly.

I nodded, watching her playful expression. She was flirting with me and it was fun.

"Hungry enough to get something to eat?" I asked her.

"Yes … I am. Let's go," she said, holding out her hand for me to take.

She was wearing a very attractive cotton top and Bermuda shorts with socks up to her knees. A pair of simple tennis shoes finished the ensemble. She looked terrific. Not overdressed and yet still exuding that class that she wore as part of her persona. It seemed natural for us to be walking hand in hand even though we had only seen each other once at the club. I felt comfortable in her presence because she made me feel that way. If she was high maintenance it didn't show.

The picnic began to break up at eight o'clock and the first bus left full. I was looking around for Rose when she walked up with Miles.

"Dex, would you mind if Miles drove me home? He doesn't live that far away from my place."

"No, not at all. I hope you had a good time," I said looking at them both.

"Very nice, Dex," she said. "And thanks again for inviting me. I really had fun today and met some really nice people."

"I'm glad. Drive carefully, Miles. I'll see you Tuesday in the office."

They wished me good night and strolled off toward the area where a few cars were parked. Miles must have brought his car, perhaps thinking he might leave early if he wasn't enjoying himself. That didn't happen.

Again, as I stood watching them walk away together, I felt a pair of hands wrap around my arm and Michelle was beside me once again.

"I'm on cleanup committee, Michelle. Can you wait for a few minutes?"

"Sure. In fact, I'll give you a hand. I don't think we have that much to do with as many helpers as we have."

We walked back to the canopy and were assigned grounds duty, having been handed each a large garden trash bag. We strolled together as we picked up the odd paper napkin, cup or plastic fork. The people had been very good about keeping the grounds tidy and there was every evidence that Dick's uncle would welcome us back next year. He seemed to enjoy the day as much as we did.

"Did you have a good time?" I asked.

"A very good time. Beautiful day, happy people, and very good company," she said, turning and smiling at me.

"I agree. I think this helped get our people to know each other a little better."

"Still playing the role of morale officer I see." I knew she was teasing.

"Can't help myself, I guess. I won't pretend I've always been like this, though."

"Oh? How were you before?"

"I don't know … a bit less social I guess. I'm not talking about the office but my personal life. We didn't have a lot of friends so we pretty much entertained ourselves."

"And that's changed since your divorce?"

"Yes. I think my time in the Caribbean turned me around. I found I was lonely … not just because I was missing my wife but I didn't have anyone I could really call a friend … a buddy. Do you understand?"

"Yes, completely. So how did you become who you are now?"

"Two very nice ladies … twin sisters. Kind of grabbed me and took care of me. It gave me something to hold on to when I was floundering."

"Were these women living on the island?"

"Yes, temporarily. They were representing the investment company that was funding the airport expansion that we had supplied the engineering for. I was on the island for eighteen months and I ended up living in their home for over a year. They are from Holland and have returned there now."

"And were you attracted to these women?"

"Yes," I answered, unselfconsciously. I didn't feel I had anything to hide from Michelle.

"And that changed you? That helped you see things differently?"

"Yes. I hadn't made up my mind what to do about my future but by the time the job was finished I found I liked who I was, liked my job and I was happy to go back to it. I also knew there would be no reconciliation with my wife. Her betrayal had been absolute. She left me nothing emotionally to want to restore."

"So … now you're divorced?"

"Almost. Another three months. I plan on celebrating Labour Day, although I guess celebration isn't quite the right word."

"And Rose was someone who you just met and clicked with?"

"Sort of. You know ... the coincidence of timing ... the right place at the right time. I was getting a little lonely so when she handed me the opportunity to spend some time with her ... I did."

"She's very grateful to you for that, you know."

"How so?"

"You made her realize she didn't have to settle for second best. She needed to get over being desperate and just be Rose."

"You learned all this in a few minutes this afternoon?"

"Dexter, I don't think you really realize just what impact you have on people ... especially women. Guys like you don't grow on trees. You don't have an arrogant bone in your body. You act like every time someone pays you a compliment it's a surprise."

"Oh. I just thought Rose needed a little cheering up. A little self-confidence, that's all."

"No ... that's a lot! Trust me, that's a lot," she said emphatically.

"Are you speaking from experience?" I asked, stopping for a moment.

"Yes ... I am. When David died, I was lost. I didn't know what to do or how to cope on my own. He was my leader in everything. I totally relied on his guidance. I didn't realize how dependent I was but I soon found out. I didn't even know how fill the gas tank on my car. I never had to do it."

"But you learned," I said, guessing.

"Yes, I did. It wasn't easy because I was trying to overcome twenty years of dependency. So you can see why I might not have been very confident in myself for a while."

"You don't act like the woman you're describing."

"Act is the right word, Dex. It is an act. I'm pretending to be the self-reliant woman in charge of her life. Janice knows better."

I was shaking my head in disbelief. If it truly was an act it was a very good one. I was beginning to feel she was looking to me to find out if there was something we could build a relationship upon. If she was as uncertain as she described, then she was telling me she wanted me to lead. I don't think she had any idea how uncertain I was. Was I getting myself in over my head?

Chapter 9
Taking a Chance

That May picnic was the beginning of a series of dates that Michelle and I enjoyed. Sometimes to a movie or play, often for dinner, occasionally for a ballgame. It was on one of those dates that there was a distinct shift in our relationship. Until then, we had held hands, kissed lightly, and generally behaved ourselves. I think we both could feel the pressure building. It changed after we had spent a pleasant evening at a local play.

We were in her late model Lincoln and I was driving. In the past, I would stop at the Rossmoor and she would drive on to her apartment. That night she had other ideas.

"Drive to my place, Dex. It's Friday, and we've got all weekend. You haven't been to my place yet and I'd like to spend some time with you," she said, placing her hand over mine.

It didn't take me any time at all to agree and head toward Lakeshore Drive. As we neared the building, Michelle took a small transmitter from her purse and pushed a button. The open grilled gate began to rise and I drove into the underground parking area as she directed me to her numbered space. The transmitter also unlocked the door to the elevator and stairs. After waiting a moment for an available car, a door slid open and we entered with Michelle inserting a card and pushing a button marked "R."

When we stepped out of the car, a large glass window was directly in front of us and I could see we were at the top of the building. To the left was 2102 and to the right, 2101. Michelle guided me right and opened the door, stepping in and turning on some lights.

It was a very nice and apparently large penthouse suite, one of two on the top floor of the building. As I looked around I saw the trappings of affluence; fine furniture, interesting artwork, and lush carpeting.

Michelle kicked off her shoes and I followed suit.

"Dex, I'm all sticky from the humidity today. I'm going to have a shower and change. Why don't you do the same, then we can relax and get to know each other better," she smiled.

I wasn't about to decline the offer and happily agreed. She led me to the main bathroom, handed me some towels and a washcloth and told me how to work the controls on the shower system. I needed the lesson. It was a multi-head system with pre-selected temperatures. The cabinet itself was almost as big as the bathroom in my apartment.

As I soaped and rinsed, I almost expected that Michelle would suddenly appear and join me, but that didn't happen. I stepped out of the shower, towelled myself off, and dressed in my slacks and shirt. I didn't bother with socks. They wouldn't be as fresh as I was so I stuffed them in my back pocket as I headed barefoot for the living area.

Waiting for Michelle, I wandered about the spacious penthouse. There was a dining area with a very nice buffet and china cabinet, along with a large period-style table and chairs. The kitchen was through a wide passage and it too was large, with a big island and plenty of cabinet and counter space. Most houses didn't have this much room.

I was just coming out of my inspection of the kitchen when Michelle reappeared and got my undivided attention. She was wearing a black silk pyjama suit, if that's what it's called. It was floor length, very sleek with material flowing from its wide legs and arms. She had a smile for me as she approached, then stopped and swirled in a circle to emphasize the graceful lines of her attire.

"You like?" she asked, already knowing my answer.

"Very nice … very elegant." I almost added very sexy. As she had moved to show off the garment it was immediately apparent that she was wearing nothing beneath it. Her nipples protruded clearly in front and her buttocks were perfectly outlined in back. I could feel my erection beginning to develop.

"Would you care for coffee … or perhaps a glass of wine or brandy?" she asked in a tempting tone.

"I'd like a glass of brandy, please."

"Oh, good. I'll have one too," she said, turning to move into the kitchen.

I followed her as if she was drawing me along. Perhaps it was the magnetic appeal of her, dressed as she was in such alluring garb. She reached up in a cupboard for the brandy bottle and I stepped behind her to help her. I was directly behind her now, touching her slightly with my hips and chest. On the spur of the moment, I did something I would never have thought I would do.

With the fingertips of my right hand, I lightly, slowly, ran them up her side, feeling her ribs as I went. Then, in a moment of complete recklessness, I moved my hand and gently cupped and stroked a fulsome breast. I felt her shiver from the contact but she didn't push me away or resist my touch. In fact, I was sure I heard a soft moan.

I couldn't see her face, but she had begun to lean back into me, the brandy bottle now forgotten. Her hands were on the countertop as if bracing her against an assault. My left hand joined the right in teasing her nipples and now her groan was more audible. Emboldened, I allowed my left hand to slip down over her abdomen and softly rub the silky smooth material of her gown.

I felt her backside push slowly back into me and she could certainly now feel my erection. I moved my hips to place my hardened member between her cheeks. She welcomed that with a swaying motion that only reinforced my hardness. One of us was going to have to do something soon.

It was Michelle who took my right hand and guided it inside her top, giving me access to her breasts. She pulled at the fold of the material and I felt a little pop as a small snap released the upper half of the garment. Still holding my hand, she slid it down to her waist where another small snap gave way and the gown parted completely.

I felt her shrug her shoulders and the lovely black item fell at her feet. She was naked before me, still facing away but leaning back more urgently against me, pressing herself into my prominent manhood. Once more, I did something I would not have thought I could attempt. I intimated with my knee that I wanted her to spread her legs and she immediately complied. She understood exactly what I was intending.

I unbuttoned my pants and they too fell at my feet, my briefs following them almost immediately. I took my cock in my hand and began to stroke her already wet centre in preparation for my entry. Again, she did everything she could to help me and within a few moments I was pushing into her. Slowly and carefully at first, but her insistence gave me courage to thrust a little more and soon I was buried well inside her.

I moved a little more forcefully and quickly as she continued to encourage me. There was absolutely no doubt in my mind that this was what she had planned all along. Her voice soon joined the action, not so much with words but with little cries of encouragement and pleasure. How long it had been since she had been with a man I did not know. I only knew she was with me now, and I was reaping the reward of her pent up need.

I leaned my head forward and captured an earlobe between my lips, then licked the back of her neck as I continued to stroke into her. In response, she threw her head back, growling a pagan, earthy moan of lust, slamming her ass back into me, the smacking sound of our joining now growing louder. This was probably going to end quite soon, but I did whatever I could to hold off as long as possible.

A few moments later her moves became more erratic and we almost fell out of rhythm as she began her orgasmic journey. I stayed with her as long as I could, but I was going to finish as well and there was nothing I could do to prevent it. I felt myself release into her once, twice, then a third time. As I did, she sagged against me and I wrapped my arms around her waist so that she didn't collapse against the granite counter or on the floor.

In all my experience, limited as it might have been, I had never had a more erotic, spontaneous coupling than this. I was in no condition to continue. Michelle was leaning back into me, breathing heavily and holding my arms tightly as they encircled her. Not a word had passed between us from the time she walked to the liquor cupboard.

I'm still not sure what got into me that night. I was either very confident of myself or very reckless. Probably the latter. Nonetheless, I picked the naked beauty up in my arms and carefully steered my way out of the kitchen toward the master bedroom. When I arrived, I saw that the bed had been turned down and I carefully laid Michelle on it crosswise with her legs dangling over the side. Her eyes were open and she was staring at me, no doubt wondering what I was doing. Still, neither of us had yet spoken.

I pulled off my shirt and now as naked as she, I got on my knees on the lushly carpeted floor, my hands gently but insistently pushing her legs apart. Again, she offered no resistance. I moved between her thighs and began to kiss the flawless, smooth skin. I was about to work my way up to the place where I had just planted my seed when I felt her hands in my hair. Was this a 'stop' or a 'go?'

I could see a bit of my semen on the lips of her vagina and I wondered what possessed me to try this. What was I trying to prove? Yet, even with that question in my head, I continued. As Michelle realized what I was planning, she must have had second thoughts. That had prompted her to place her hands on my head again, trying to decide if she should put a stop to my intentions. As I made up my mind to continue, I felt her resistance lessen.

I moved toward my target and slowly, with the flat of my tongue, I began to make love to her once again. This was going to be a very different kind of penetration. I had plenty of experience with oral sex but none just after I had planted my seed inside a woman. It was too late to stop now, and Michelle was making no sign that she wanted me to.

In fact, I was bringing her back to life with my tongue and fingers. Her hips were rising and falling erratically, responding to whatever stimuli she felt. Her grip on my head tightened and I could feel her fingers in my hair. She was holding on tight, her body dancing to whatever music my tongue created. I flicked the tip of her clitoris and got the response I expected. Her hips snapped up in reaction.

I was beginning to tire … or at least my tongue was. Michelle was nearing another orgasm and I willed myself to continue. At last she let go and I could stop and rest. I crawled up beside her, lying on my back. She rolled over me and gave me a deep, soulful kiss. Whatever I had accomplished, she approved of it. I wondered if it was something her late husband had not provided.

We lay there for a while, her head on my shoulder, our legs dangling over the edge of the bed. I kissed her forehead and ran my fingers through her soft, flowing hair. Her hand was holding my now flaccid cock, not manipulating it, just holding it lightly.

"That was wonderful," she said at last. "I didn't realize just how much I wanted you and you were perfect for me."

"We took some chances tonight," I said. "That gown didn't leave much to the imagination."

"It was either that or I would just come out naked. It was a coin toss."

"Were you worried I wouldn't get the message?"

"That thought did cross my mind. I can never be sure just what you are thinking about when it comes to women, Dex. Sometimes shy, but tonight a completely different person. You took command and I was the lucky one when you did."

"You were irresistible. I'm sure that was your plan, wasn't it? Well, it worked. I couldn't resist you, so everything that happened was a result of that."

"You'll stay tonight, won't you?"

"Yes. You might regret it in the morning, but I do want to stay. I want to wake up with you."

"We've started something, haven't we?" It was as much a statement as a question.

"I hope so. Is that what you want?" I wondered.

"Yes. As little as I know about you, as little time as I've known you, everything I've learned tells me that you are right for me."

"Well, we're going to have some time to find out so let's enjoy ourselves and see where it goes. I'm not a one-night-stand kind of guy. I'm looking for something more than that."

"You wouldn't be in this apartment tonight if I thought otherwise. But now that you're here, I'm going to keep you here as long as I can."

After a few minutes, Michelle rose and padded to the ensuite bathroom, closing the door behind her. She returned a minute or so later and crawled on top of me, rubbing my still limp cock with her lightly haired sex. I began to respond to her tantalizing little game and she noticed.

"Oh … isn't that nice. Can I have some more please, sir?"

"Of course you may. Just tell me your heart's desire, young lady, and I'll try and fulfill your wishes."

"Well, after that glorious fucking you gave me in the kitchen, I think I'd like you to make love to me. Something nice and slow and lasting."

"How would you like me to start? A little foreplay, perhaps?"

"I think I've had all the foreplay I can handle tonight, Dex. I'm still carrying some of you around in me and what I really want is to have you inside me again."

I sat up and moved myself to one side of the big bed and invited Michelle to join me.

"I want you on top," I whispered. "I want to see you as you ride me. You can decide how fast or how slow."

She mounted me; her legs straddling me while her hand found my now erect cock and placed it at her entrance. She slowly pushed down on me and I slipped into her for the second time. It was just as superb as the first time. She moved to put her hands beside my head and waved her wonderfully full breasts in front of my mouth.

I couldn't resist. I nipped at them as they swayed back and forth, eventually catching one between my lips, tonguing the nipple to its aroused hardness. She pulled it away from me and offered the other breast for my pleasure. All the while, she was slowly rising and falling on my rigid member, clearly enjoying the sensations I was creating in both areas of her body.

The slowly measured pace she had chosen was inspired, sensual and very satisfying. Her eyes were closed some of the time as I watched her move over me. She was finding fulfillment at her own pace, perhaps in some dream world she had created. I moved my hands from her hips to her breasts and used my thumbs to gently stroke her small, pink nipples. I was rewarded with groans and hums of pleasure from her.

There was never a moment of urgency. It was like a slowly growing wave as it approached the shore, not crashing onto the beach but unfurling as it arrived, gently, quietly. Michelle smiled, probably to herself. I could see it on her lips and in her eyes when they were open. This was pure pleasure and not to be hurried but stretched out for as long as possible.

When we finished, I was spent … physically and mentally. This evening had been an unexpected, wonderful surprise. Better yet, I felt this was the beginning of something more meaningful for me. I didn't take her sexual surrender lightly. I had been chosen and I accepted that with the choice came responsibility. I wondered if she knew just how much I had found contentment with her. It was a completely different feeling from the twins.

I awoke with my arm on Michelle's thigh and my face buried in her silken hair. The scent of a sleeping woman had always been an aphrodisiac to me and this morning was no exception. I was aroused and I'm sure if Michelle had been awake, she would have known it. Once again, my erection was nicely tucked between the cheeks of her lovely bottom.

Her arms were crossed in front of her denying me access to her breasts but it didn't matter. I was content to lie here in complete comfort as she slept. My hand found the smooth, soft skin of her tummy and without intent I found I was stroking her gently. At length, she stirred and rolled onto her back. Again my hand rested on her thigh, close to her naked centre.

I assumed she was in the process of waking. Her knees came up and her hands were between her thighs. She found my hand and I felt hers close over it, squeezing it gently. I watched her face for signs of waking and saw her eyelids begin to flutter. She groaned, letting her knees fall to the bed, her eyes now beginning to open.

I placed my hand back on her upper thigh, massaging it lightly. She was awake now but I guessed she was disoriented. Who was in her bed? It must have come to her and she turned to me, smiling as she realized she was right.

"G'mornin' Dex," she whispered with a yawn.

"Mornin' Michelle. Sleep well?'

"Yes … very well. Very nice dreams. Very sexy dreams," she said with a sleepy smile.

I touched her cheek with my fingertips, slowly drawing them toward her mouth. She opened and took them in, sucking lightly on them. Her hand took mine, holding it first before taking it to her breast. My thumb once again stroked the areola and nipple and she responded with a moan of pleasure. I think we might have lain there for several hours if it weren't for the call of nature. First Michelle, and then me. I borrowed some of her mouthwash and then quickly returned to the bed. We laughed when we discovered each of us had done the same thing. Then we kissed a long, soft, tender kiss, one more accustomed to familiar lovers. It seemed just the right thing that morning.

Her hand found my growing erection and she softly gripped and stroked it to life. I was fairly sure she'd need some lubrication and I moved to create some with my tongue once more.

"Oh, God yes, Dex," she cried as I began.

She had gone from a sleepy, languid state to arousal within seconds as I worked my tongue and fingers on her labia and, after a while, her clit. She was moving her hips and gripping my head just as she had done the evening before. Her response was becoming more urgent and I could sense she wanted me to enter her soon.

I kissed and licked my way up her lovely, mature body until I reached her mouth where we locked onto each other with an almost desperate passion. And again she took me in hand and guided me into her, insistent on my satisfying her need. I thought I would repeat the pace we had finished with last night but after a few minutes Michelle became much more demanding.

"More ... please ... more," she cried, driving her hips upward at me.

I was sure I wouldn't last very long but it was what she wanted and I strived to meet her demand. I increased my stroke and pace and she reacted by grabbing my arms near the shoulders and rising even more insistently toward me. We were banging together at a furious rate that neither of us could sustain. I was at the breaking point and without much more than a strangled cry, I let go.

I stayed as long as I could but soon enough I began to wilt. Drops of perspiration were falling on Michelle's head but she didn't seem to notice or care. At last, with one final lunge, she finished just as I was about to withdraw. Only luck could account for our timing.

We lay beside each other, panting as we came down from the high of our release. This was all new territory for me. Neither the twins nor my ex-wife were ever this demanding. Michelle was a completely different woman from the cultured, elegant lady I believed her to be. If this was what I had to look forward to in a middle-age love affair, I was going to have to prepare myself. A few more workouts in the exercise room were in order.

She was a woman of few words in the bedroom. No passionate cries of pleasure or crude demands. No empty love words in the heat of the moment. Her body in action was the voice that spoke of her approval. She rolled toward me once more, placing her hand on my cheek, gazing into my eyes.

"You make me feel very young, Dexter. It's a very nice feeling that I haven't experienced in a long time. I think we are very good together, don't you?"

"Yes. Very good. But right now, I think we both need a shower. And as far as I can remember my clothes are still in the kitchen," I chuckled.

"There's no one to peek through the windows so you can walk around naked all day if you like," she grinned. "I'll put your clothes in the wash and they'll be fresh and clean in an hour. In the meantime, if you insist on covering yourself up, there's a robe on the back of the bathroom door you can use."

"I thought you'd be kicking me out by now."

"What! Whatever gave you that idea? If I had my way you'd be moving in with me today."

"Might be a little soon for that, don't you think."

"Maybe. Let's give it a week," she laughed.

"I might have some bad habits you may not appreciate?"

"Somehow I doubt that, but I'll correct them as we go. Perhaps you just need a strong hand to guide you."

"Like the hand that you used last night and this morning?"

She laughed. "Yes. Exactly like that."

Chapter 10
Cohabitation

I have to admit that I was somewhat distracted at work the following week. Thankfully, Terry and Petra had a good handle on the training and I wasn't really needed. If anyone knew I was involved with Michelle, they didn't say anything. It wasn't as if I was trying to hide from it, but then again, I wasn't advertising that I was intimate with one of the partners.

She called me at work to invite me to the theatre and dinner. We settled on my meeting her at her place and then taking a cab. The tickets were for Friday night and it was a given that I would stay over at her penthouse. At least, it was a given for Michelle. Who was I to fight it? I'd take an overnight bag with a change for Saturday and a backup for Sunday.

The play, a well-worn Agatha Christie mystery, was a delight. The actors, if not British, certainly had their parts down pat in the appropriate vernacular. The setting had been updated from the Victorian era to the nineties and the dialogue was a good deal more risqué, but it was never vulgar and it was consistently good. We were in high spirits when we walked from the theatre to the nearby restaurant.

I was more and more aware of just how comfortable I found myself in Michelle's company. She was a big part of that, of course. I never felt I had to behave in a certain way to live up to her expectations. She didn't act the part of the rich socialite. I couldn't imagine that she ever did, despite some of the company she and her late husband might have kept. She was a natural as the girl next door whoever that might be.

It was nearing midnight when we arrived back at her apartment. I wasn't tired, in fact the opposite. The evening had been a real tonic and Michelle was showing no signs of fatigue either. As I closed the door behind me, she slipped into my arms and kissed me. It seemed so completely natural that we would be here. I didn't feel any hesitation in responding to her or accepting that we belonged together.

We made love, that natural, quiet, flowing act of joining that you long for but don't always experience. It seemed to have lasted quite a long while but I wasn't keeping track and I really didn't care. It was so easy and satisfying that I didn't want it to end.

"Will you move in here?" she asked as we lay in the afterglow.

"Do you want me to?" I asked stupidly.

"No ... or course not," she laughed. "You fool, Dex. Of course, I want you to. I want you all to myself every night."

"Then I will. But it does ask a question."

"What question?"

"What happens when my assignment is finished?"

"Will that be soon?"

"The truth? For all intents and purposes, I'm done now. Everything we wanted to accomplish at Trent is in place. The business is going to be fine now. Rueben will be a good general manager and Terry and Petra will make sure the design department stays on course. Janice, of course, will continue to be Janice. Wolf is already generating new work, so I'd say I'm pretty well finished."

"But you're still here."

"I don't have another assignment and Dorothy has done a great job taking over for me in Vancouver. I'm thinking I might take a vacation if Tom doesn't have something for me. In the meantime, I've sold my home and my car and aside from my daughter, I have nothing to call me back to the west coast. I have enough money to live comfortably for some time."

"But you'd move in with me anyway?" she tested.

"If you're serious about us, yes."

"Does that mean *you're* serious about us?" She seemed uncertain about my decision.

"Yes. I know we haven't known each other for very long, but something about how we connect makes this very different from a normal 'getting to know you' relationship. If you're willing, I want to find out just where we can go with this."

She looked at me intently, studying my face, her eyes unblinking.

"I want that too. You're right, this is all happening very quickly, but like you, something about it feels right. In fact, it feels natural … as if we've known each other for a long time. Strange, isn't it?"

"Very strange … but all good from my point of view," I smiled.

I moved my few belongings to the Penthouse the next afternoon and cancelled the lease. I was now a "kept man."

It was too nice a weekend to spend it entirely in bed so we took Michelle's car and drove around the metropolitan Toronto area, just sightseeing and spending time together. I thought that's what we needed … time together. If I had any nagging doubt, it was related to how quickly all this was happening. We'd known each other little over a month since the picnic. It still felt right, but nevertheless, my generally conservative nature was holding me back.

We were sitting in a little Bistro Saturday evening, having a light supper when Michelle decided it was time to tell me more about herself and her marriage to David Gauthier.

"My maiden name is Catchpole. I hated it. I can still remember some of the taunts of my schoolmates. So, I am happy with my married name. I married David when I was just twenty-one and able to do as I wished and not as my mother demanded. I was the only daughter in a family of five. My two brothers are older and we don't see each other very much. Martin lives in Montreal, and Michael lives in Calgary.

"Martin is gay and has a live-in lover whom I've only met once. We get along fine but we don't have much in common. He's a graphic artist and does quite well, I understand. Michael is married with one son and works in the oil industry. I don't know exactly what he does but apparently he's fairly high up in his firm. He takes after mother in many ways. So both my brothers are successes."

She stopped for a moment, and I saw a far away look for a few seconds before she returned to her narrative.

"David was a very dynamic personality. He had a clear vision of what he wanted when he graduated from university and he set about achieving it, dragging me along with him."

"Dragging?" I quizzed.

"Virtually. His ambition to own his own civil engineering and consulting firm consumed him first and foremost. He worked long hours and was relentless in achieving his partnership in Trent. When he did, I thought things would calm down a little and we could live a normal life, but it wasn't to be. 'Success breeds success' he would chant.

"When things started to decline at Trent, he worked even harder, as if he could turn it around by himself. He couldn't, of course, but it didn't stop him from throwing all his energy into trying. It finally killed him. He had a brain aneurism one morning at the office and he was dead before his head hit the desk.

"I grieved. He wasn't the ideal husband. He wasn't there all the time, emotionally or physically. But he was true and faithful and dedicated to us, the boys and me. He just didn't have enough time for us. I hated Trent for what it did to him but, in a way, I understood how he could be obsessed with its success. It was all part of his original plan for the future. He made an awful lot of money and yet never got to enjoy it."

"And that was three years ago?"

"Almost. It seems like yesterday at times and at other times it seems like ancient history. I suppose it depends on my mood. Since you've come along, I haven't been dwelling on the past. In fact, I've been thinking about the future, just like you have," she smiled.

"You said you have two sons. Where are they?"

"Carter works for his Uncle Michael in Calgary and I'm told he's on his way up. He's a chemical engineer, which upset his father. David was sure Carter would take up civil engineering and follow in his footsteps. I think Carter is a little better balanced than David was at that age.

"Our other son, Kyle, is single and living in Montgomery, Alabama. He works for a big paper company in their development department. They specialize in making products from recycled paper so they are high on the 'good guy' list with the environmental people. Kyle says it's a good thing most of the advocacy groups don't know much about the recycling processes. They wouldn't be quite so supportive," she grinned.

"So your family is spread around then," I said. "Are your parents still alive?"

"Yes. My mother and father are divorced. Dad couldn't handle Mother's manipulative ways any longer and they split up after I married. He lives on the beach in Amherstburg, not far from Windsor-Detroit. He loves it there and has a girlfriend that lives with him.

"My mother and I don't see each other at all. She and I don't get along and haven't since I married David. In her opinion, I married 'beneath myself.' Sounds very English, doesn't it? Well, no surprise, my mother is English and still clings to the old class system."

"So ... you've been alone since David died?"

She nodded. "I thought for a while that I probably would be alone for the rest of my life. I don't know why. I'm forty-eight, hardly dowager material," she smiled. "I had been thinking about getting out and trying to find a new life for myself, whatever that means. I had become interested in the fate of Trent Engineering when Tom Yardley and Wolf called to invite me to discuss a merger. I thought it was important to get myself up to date quickly.

"John Flannery rejected the idea of course, but I knew that if he was the only dissenter, Rueben, Dick and I could out-vote him. I'm not dependent on Trent for my future, but I wouldn't want to see it fail so why not get involved? I'm glad I did. It gave me a sense of purpose; something to preserve what David had worked so hard to build.

"Your principals were very nice men and, with the exception of John, we all got along very well. When they made their proposal, John stomped out of the room claiming he'd never agree to anything that would hand over control to a 'bunch of cowboys.' It would have been funny if you didn't know what was eating at him.

"Rueben, Dick and I met privately and discussed the proposal. In reality, we knew we couldn't save Trent by ourselves. We needed help and Pinecone offered that help. In addition, we were offered autonomy to run the business in a manner appropriate to the values of the old Trent organization. Naturally, we needed to coordinate the accounting, design and administration, but the Trent name would be preserved because it had value. It took us very little time to decide that this was in the best interests of both ourselves and our employees.

"John, of course, was livid. We had outvoted him and he took it personally. But we stuck to our guns and the merger/acquisition went through. We were no longer the majority partners but we weren't an afterthought. Besides, all our background checks on Tom and Wolf came up the same. They are talented, aggressive and honest. They do what they say they are going to do and are well respected in the community. Your competitors spoke highly of Pinecone, which counted for a lot as well.

"Then, the next thing I hear is Janice telling me there's a new sheriff in town and he's making changes. Good changes. You had her on your side right from the get-go. I think that's what intrigued me about you in the first place. Janice isn't some silly girl who's easily swayed by a handsome man. So, after her mentioning three or four times what you were doing and how well you were doing it, I decided to find out just who this Dexter McLeod character was," she smiled.

"So, what did you think when you walked into the University Club that day?" I asked.

"I thought I had the wrong table. You didn't look anything like the mental picture I had of a computer guy. In fact, you looked like a professional businessman, completely at home in that club. It was then I realized what Janice had been telling me."

"Oh ... and just what had Janice been telling you?"

"She said, and I quote, 'You've got to meet this guy. He's a stud.'"

I laughed. "I'll have to remember to thank Janice for being so generous with her praise."

"So here we are," I added after a quiet moment.

"Your turn," she said. "I know some things about you but not an awful lot."

"Well, we have some things in common. I have a son in Chile … he's a mining engineer and a daughter in Vancouver who's an interior designer. Both are in their early twenties. I was born in Vancouver and went to school at BCIT, the technical college. I was one of the first graduates on CADD systems so I got in on the ground floor. From there, I got on with Tom and Wolf not long after they started up and I've been there ever since.

"Most of the changes in my life have happened within the last two years. I found out my wife was cheating on me and planned to leave me and take whatever she could get her hands on. I was very angry and took some preventative measures to mess up her plans."

"That doesn't tell me much, Dex. What prompted her to do that?"

"I don't know and I don't think she does either. It wasn't hormone imbalance or drugs or any of the other usual medical excuses. She's undergoing psychological therapy and maybe that will get to the bottom of it but it won't make any difference. Her actions were so cold-blooded over a year than I can't bring myself to excuse anything she did. Having an affair was one thing. Planning to take every dollar she could from me was quite another."

"But that was two years ago, Dex. Your divorce is only going through now. What happened?"

"I ran. I didn't want Sandra and her lover to succeed so I concocted a plan to minimize the damage and ran. Tom helped me by making it look like I had quit Pinecone and disappeared. In fact, I was the site rep at one of our projects in the Caribbean."

"I take it your plan worked?"

"Yes … but in the end, it wasn't really necessary. Turned out her lover was embezzling funds from some of his clients and was arrested and charged. That put an end to their grand scheme."

"But you said you had no regrets about leaving," Michelle reminded me.

"I don't. It was the best thing for me. It let me get my head around what had happened and what I might do about myself in the future. So when the job was done, I went back to Vancouver to settle things. Sandra hadn't initiated a divorce so it was up to me. To make a long story short, I made her an offer and she accepted it."

"Are you still angry with her?"

"Yes … from time to time. She destroyed something that I thought was good. She took away my beliefs and my personal foundation. I knew almost right away that I could never take her back. The two years since has been a relief. I got my self-esteem back and my confidence. It didn't hurt that Tom and Wolf had my promotion and this job for me. Then … you came along."

"And I'm good for you too?" she asked, putting her hand over mine.

"You know it. I'm still amazed at how quickly we have come together. I'm trying to understand how I could do what I did that evening in your kitchen. There's nothing in my makeup that could account for my behaviour that night. But … having said that … I have no regrets. Not any more."

"Good. I don't want you to have regrets. I'm glad you took me the way you did. It changed what I thought about you. You weren't shy and yet you weren't some guy who thought he could do what he wanted with me. It made you a bit mysterious in a way. You somehow knew what I wanted … needed … at that moment. I wanted to be taken and you did."

"Completely out of character for me but … looking back … I don't have any second thoughts," I admitted.

"Neither do I," she smiled faintly. "It was perfect. Afterwards was just as perfect. In some way, we link our desires. I don't quite know how, but it doesn't really matter, does it?"

"It only matters that we do communicate," I agreed. "We don't say much when we make love, but we seem to understand each other's wants very well."

"I'm going to want to explore that special kind of communication," she teased. "I think we need a good deal more experience, don't you?"

"Now that you mention it, I agree. We do have a lot to learn about each other."

"What have you decided to do about your job?"

"I'll phone Tom on Monday and let him know I'm almost finished here. He'll be happy. I'm almost two months ahead of his schedule and that will keep us under budget. He'll let me know if he has another assignment for me. If not, I'm thinking vacation with a very nice companion. How does the south of France sound?"

"I've never been there. I'd love to go, especially with you. But what if Tom has another project for you?"

"Maybe you'd like to come along with me if it's not in some hell-hole. I really don't want to lose you this quickly. I'm hoping Tom will understand."

"Why don't you let me decide if it's a hell-hole," she smiled. "Besides, I can't see Tom or Wolf treating their most valuable Vice President that way."

"We'll find out quick enough. In the meantime, I plan to spend as much time with you as you can stand."

"I have a very high tolerance threshold for you," she boasted with another of her genuine smiles.

~~***~~

I called Tom on Monday morning just after ten. I had a question to ask and some explaining to do.

"Hey, Dex. So how was your weekend?"

"Very nice, Tom. About as nice as it could be."

"Oh … that sounds interesting. Should I assume there's a lady involved?"

"Of course. What else would cheer up an about-to-be divorced guy living in a strange city?"

"Should I also assume that the lady in question is one of our shareholders?" he chuckled.

"Can't fool you, can I. Yes … I moved in with Michelle this weekend. If you were looking to define a whirlwind romance, this would be it."

"So … what's your plan?"

"That's what I was calling you about. What's *your* plan?"

"I'm happy with the way things are, Dex. You are handling the situation in Toronto perfectly. If you want to stay and supervise the whole operation that would be great with both me and Wolf."

"I don't think that's going to work, Tom. Rueben and Dick are both major shareholders, unlike me. As much as we get along very well, I can't see myself being their boss."

"Okay, time for the facts of life, Dex. Rueben and Dick are both engineers, like Wolf and me. They are busy with their day-to-day jobs and don't really appreciate or have time for the administrative side. I have it on good authority that they would welcome someone to take that burden off them and that unnamed person would get their full cooperation."

"Unnamed?"

"Well ... to be truthful ... they did mention your name as the one person they would be most comfortable with."

"So ... this is a set-up ... right?"

"Well ... I wouldn't put it quite that way ... but I guess you might see it in that light."

He had me laughing at the transparency of this ploy. He knew about Michelle. He knew that the project's status was, for all intents and purposes, complete. There could only be one source: Janice. On top of that, he knew I would only accept the new post if Rueben and Dick agreed. I guess that's why he's the boss.

"Would you mind if I took some time off before I started my new assignment?"

"I think you've earned a nice vacation, Dex. Take that lady of yours with you and have some fun in the sun. Meanwhile, Wolf and I will dream up some work for you when you get back."

"Thanks, Tom. I'll let you know my plans as soon as they are finalized."

I hung up and immediately called Michelle.

"Looks like I'm going to be resident in Toronto for the foreseeable future. Tom wants me to take over the corner office and apparently I have Rueben and Dick's blessing."

"Wonderful!" she exclaimed. "But what about that holiday?"

"Why don't you start planning one and I'll make myself available."

"Perfect! The south of France, right?"

"Maybe we should talk about this when I get home," I suggested.

"Home? This is home for you?" She sounded taken aback.

"Oh ... uhhm ... am I being presumptuous?"

"No ... No! You just surprised me, that's all. I didn't expect you would think of this as your home. I mean ... it is ... but ... I guess I have to get used to the idea," she stammered.

I chuckled at her discomfort. I had used a long familiar term for wherever I lived and I caught her off guard.

"If we are going to live together, then it will be home," I said simply.

"Yes ... it will be ... won't it." She was beginning to recover from my comment.

"Are you uncomfortable with my being there?"

"No!" she said immediately. "No ... I'm very happy that you're here. I'm just trying to get used to the idea that I won't be alone any more. I don't think I quite believe it yet."

"When I show up sometime before six o'clock, will that be proof enough?"

"Yes," she giggled, finally seeing the humour in our conversation. "Just don't waltz in here with 'Honey, I'm home,' please."

"I can't. I don't have a key and you'll have to supply the elevator code."

"Oh ... I didn't even think of that. I'll deal with that this afternoon."

"Then can I say 'Honey, I'm home?'"

"No ... I refuse to be June Cleaver," she laughed.

We ended the conversation with my having to get back to work and promising to be home before six.

When we hung up, I realized neither of us had said "I love you" yet. I thought about it for a while and knew we weren't there yet. We were somewhere between like and love. Whether we got to love was yet to be determined.

Chapter 11
The New Order

It felt quite strange walking into the office on Monday morning. I was expected to inhabit the corner office, the same office John Flannery had occupied. It was a given that John would not be returning from his leave. As usual, I was the first to arrive and that gave me an opportunity to scout his office more thoroughly. I had assumed that much of John's things and files would still be there but that didn't turn out to be the case.

At some point the office had been cleaned and emptied of any of Flannery's personal files and memorabilia. Whether he had done it himself or had someone do it for him, I didn't know. It seemed barren and cold now with nothing at all to personalize it. I thought it would be a good idea to remedy that and I was thinking Michelle could help me.

A set of keys was hanging from the lock on the centre desk drawer and I removed them. A second key fit the filing cabinet and a third fit a set of cabinet doors built into the wall. When I opened it, I found a well stocked bar with a refrigerator and sink to complement it. It would appear that the previous resident could host a nice little reception if he was in the mood.

I stood gazing out over the view of the Toronto skyline and lakeshore. Not quite as dramatic as Vancouver, but very nice as well. I knew from my conversations with Tom that Trent owned the floor on which we were situated and it must be worth a fortune in today's commercial real estate market.

As I looked around, I realized that this office was too pretentious for me. I was a pretender in this new role. There was no doubt in my mind that Terry could handle the management of the design department. He had the maturity and now the experience to accept the responsibility. So what was I to do?

I was sitting in the big leather chair behind the desk, lost in my thoughts when I became aware I was not alone.

"Good morning, Dex. I see you've found your new office," Janice said with a smile.

I shook my head. "I'm not comfortable here, Janice. I feel like a fraud. I'm nothing more than a trumped up designer pretending to be a general manager. I'll be out of touch way back here."

"I don't know where else you could go, Dex."

"I was thinking about the meeting room. It isn't as big as this room. We could swap places and make this the meeting room. That way I'd be more visible and the meetings would be in a quiet, well lit area."

"Are you sure about this?" she asked, her brow wrinkled.

"Nope, but I know I'm not comfortable back here. Too isolated. You know me by now. I like to be where the action is. You can't do that back here, tucked away. The only things we'd have to move would be the table and chairs from the meeting room and the desk, file cabinet and chair from here. The meeting room has a big window so it won't be like I'm stuck in some cave."

"You're the boss, Dex. I guess I can see your point. You are a lot more social than the previous occupant," she grinned.

"Can you arrange with someone to get it done? In the meantime, I'll stay where I am until that's accomplished. Brigit can deal with the telephone switch I imagine," I said looking around.

"I'll call the building superintendent. He takes care of that kind of thing."

"Thanks. One other thing. I haven't met the person in charge of accounting. Who is that?"

"Well, technically, no one. Our last manager quit to take another job. That was almost six months ago. John didn't want him replaced and left it to me to make sure the work was done on time. For now, Teresa Tremonte is looking after getting the work coordinated and filed. She sends her information to Vancouver now. I don't know any more than that.

"I'm no accountant, Dex. Just like you, I'm doing the best I can without the credentials to know if everything's okay. So far the auditors have been satisfied, but they're due back in a couple of months so things could change."

"Damn!" I spat. "What the hell was John thinking? Running this place without financial guidance is a recipe for disaster. There's only so much you can cut back before you can't function. Is Teresa capable of running the department?"

Janice shrugged and I should have known that was coming. She was in no position to make a judgment.

I was frustrated. Everywhere I turned the so-called economies had turned into problems that needed addressing. My phone call to Tom was going to be a lengthy one this afternoon.

Janice was watching me and I'm sure she could hear the gears grinding.

"You'll figure it out, Dex. Do what you think is right. Tell Tom what you want to do and why. That's all you can do."

Janice was right. If Tom rejected my plan, I'd have to go back and see what alternatives I could come up with. Right now, my new number one priority was to establish some management in accounting.

"Thanks, Janice. You're right of course. Now, let's get the coffee started."

Terry arrived a few minutes later, choosing to adopt the earlier start in the design department. I called him into my office and closed the door.

"Terry, sometime this morning there will be an announcement that I have been appointed General Manager of Trent Engineering. This is being done with the knowledge and approval of Rueben and Dick," I said, stopping to see his reaction.

"Great. I think that's great. You're just the guy for the job, Dex," he said sincerely.

I relaxed a bit. "As a result, you will be promoted to Manager of Design, effective immediately. Your pay will increase accordingly by twenty percent and you will continue to report to me. I suggest you discuss this with Petra to let her know that she would be next in line and that she shouldn't be discouraged that she didn't get the job. I don't expect a problem but I think you should acknowledge that she's your right hand and that she should expect a raise as well, although not as large as yours. She will be in charge in your absence. I will talk to her as well. Any questions?"

"Yes. When did all this happen? I didn't have a clue any of this was going on."

"No ... I understand. You and Petra have been an important element in getting this department back to where it had to be. Your cooperation and support has shown me that you both are going to be invaluable in the growth of Trent. My work is essentially done as far as that project goes. Rueben has let it be known that he didn't want the administrative responsibility so he'll be Manager of Engineering Services but senior to you."

"Oh boy, this is a surprise. When will this be announced?"

"This morning. Rueben and Dick already know, as does Janice. So it's really a matter of informing the rest of the staff. We'll get everyone together at ten o'clock in the meeting room and make a couple of announcements. Until then, please just keep it between you and Petra for the time being."

"Yes ... of course. Is it all right if I call my wife? She'll be really excited when she hears."

"Sure," I said, pleased at his enthusiasm. I stood and walked around the desk, holding out my hand. Terry took it and we shook heartily. "Congratulations, Terry. You've earned this."

I started plotting my move to the new office if for no other reason than to give myself something to do for the next two hours. Janice stopped in to tell me that the men would be in to move the furniture sometime after eleven that morning. Brigit was asked to inform the staff of the general meeting in the "old" meeting room at ten.

I could see a lot of question marks on faces until we had everyone in the room just after ten o'clock.

"You all know that Trent Engineering has been undergoing a substantial facelift in the past few weeks," I began. "Your cooperation and energy has made that project go better and sooner than anyone expected. For that, the partners want you to know how grateful they are and wish to thank you in a tangible way.

"First of all, the wage freeze has been lifted." There was a general voice of approval with that announcement.

"Secondly, we are beginning to hire new staff as we obtain more business for the firm." Again, sounds of approval.

"I also want to make some personnel announcements. First, Rueben Golowitz is Manager of Engineering, as you already knew. Janice Meriwether will continue as Manager of Administration, and I'm pleased to announce that Terry Sanderson has been appointed Manager of Design.

Congratulations, Terry," I said, and there was a round of applause. Apparently I had made a popular decision.

"A decision on a Manager of Accounting Services will be announced in due course," I added vaguely.

"I have been asked to assume the role of General Manager," I continued. "I promise to be accessible and visible as long as I am here. Naturally, Rueben will be in charge in my absence. I will be moving the office to this room later this morning. The new meeting room will be the corner office that so few of you ever visited," I chuckled.

I was about to say something when someone began to clap, and within a few seconds, everyone seemed to be applauding. I was surprised and very happy that my appointment had been accepted so well. I breathed another sigh of relief. We were off to a good start.

I had a number of people stop by the office and congratulate me and thank me for helping Trent "get back on its feet." I just hoped I could keep the momentum going in the right direction for the next while.

Reuben and Dick stopped by and insisted they take me to lunch. I quickly agreed.

"I like your meetings, Dex," Reuben said with a grin. "They're short, to the point and leave everyone feeling good. That's a big change from the last regime."

"Good news meetings are always easier than bad news ones, Reuben. I'm just happy we have the support of the staff, particularly you and Dick. You guys and your staff are the engine that makes this place work. The rest of us don't have a job without you."

"The attitude around the office is so much different from before," Dick observed. "Our guys are much more into their jobs now that they don't have layoffs or cutbacks hanging over their heads. Wolf is really good at finding work, isn't he?"

"Yes. Very good. He'll do everything he can to keep us hopping around here. But I wanted to ask you about contact with some of the local architects and contractors. Who looked after that in the past?"

"David Gauthier," Dick answered. "He was a real go-getter. He could schmooze with the best of them. When he died our contacts dropped off and in the end, we really didn't have any. I think that's something we need to address if we want Trent to restore its local reputation."

"I agree," Reuben chimed in.

"Okay, that's at the top of my agenda. Any suggestions?"

The two men looked at each other, apparently uncomfortable with a response. Finally, Reuben spoke.

"Stop me if I'm on sensitive territory here, Dex. David and Michelle were a good team on the social scene. I think Michelle might have brought in as many opportunities as he did. I was wondering ... if you and Michelle are okay with it ... you might think about re-establishing contacts that she had in the past."

"No need to tiptoe, guys. Michelle and I are living together and I'm not trying to keep it a secret. So ... let me talk to her and see how she feels about it. I'm not an engineer, so I'm going to have to take a different approach. I'll have to get some advice on that from Wolf and Tom as well as you two."

"Anytime, Dex," Reuben said quickly. "You'll get our full cooperation. You've done a great job so far and I can see you and Michelle being a very effective force together."

"Well, first things first. I have to get her to agree that it's a good idea," I smiled.

"I'm betting that won't take too much convincing," Dick said. "I got the impression watching her that she enjoyed the role. Good luck."

By the time we got back to the office the furniture had been moved and my phone and computer installed. I went in and sat down, looking around the room. There were a number of photos on the wall, undoubtedly of past projects at Trent. Janice had arranged to have my files moved from the design department office to my new, giant desk.

She had instructed the movers to place the desk at the end of the room with the windows on the right. That would reduce the glare on the computer screen. Sun shades would look after the view to the south during the spring and summer months. When I looked around, I had taken up barely a third of the space available.

"Janice, there's a table in the other open office that doesn't seem to be used. What is it for?" I asked.

"Lately, that's where the auditors have been housed. Why do you ask?"

"I think I'd like to have it in my office for smaller meetings and planning sessions. Right now I feel like I'm wasting useful space. If we can round up four comfortable chairs, it would help make the office friendlier."

"Sure. I can get a couple of the guys to move it this afternoon. Won't take but a few minutes."

"Thanks. I wanted to talk about a suggestion Reuben and Dick had today. They were talking about Michelle, and maybe me, re-establishing contact with the architects and contractors that her husband had developed. It would be a proactive move to find some more business and get Trent's name back in front of these people. What's your opinion?"

"I think that's a hell of an idea. She knows who to talk to and how to get appointments so it's a natural. You can handle the P.R. part easily, Dex. It isn't knowing all about engineering, it's about giving them the confidence that Trent is back to where it was before David passed. That and the improvements you've made will make a huge difference."

"That's good to hear. I'm a little reluctant to be the face of Trent Engineering but Michelle could pull that off no problem from what you're telling me."

"I'm sure of it. I like the idea that we're going to look after ourselves and not wait for someone else to find business," she said with a positive nod of her head.

"Did David ever bring any of the clients in for a tour of the offices?"

"Yes, once in a while. He wasn't that familiar with the design department but he usually did the tour just before taking them to lunch at the University Club. That usually impressed them too."

"I forgot to ask. Is that a corporate membership?"

"Yes. John pretty much made it off limits when things started to go downhill but I can easily get you recommended for an associate membership on Michelle's say-so. In the meantime, you can use her membership."

"Good. Anything else I should know?" I asked.

"Well, since the salary freeze is off, I'd better get you a salary review schedule and you, Rueben, and Terry can get started on what needs to be done. I'll look after my end of the business. Your responsibility is only for the managers but they will have to bring all the reviews and recommendations through you for final approval."

"Fine, that's the way it should work. In the meantime, I'll get with Tom and discuss what we can do and when we can do it."

I couldn't put it off any longer and called Vancouver to talk to Tom. An hour later, I had two pages of notes and the outline of a plan to handle the immediate problems.

"There's no doubt you can't continue without adequate accounting supervision," Tom said. "The previous controller quit right in the middle of our negotiations and wasn't replaced. The young woman they assigned to handle the load reported to Janice but I don't think she was ready to take over as manager. You have two choices. Pick one from the Vancouver operation that could handle the job, or hire locally. My suggestion is the latter. We can get him or her up to speed with our procedures fairly quickly with one of our people on loan for a week or so."

"Okay. I'll get an advertisement ready ASAP. Shall I use the previous person's salary as a guide?"

"Sure. You might have to pay more but I'll leave that to your judgment. The former man quit because he could get a job for more money and less hassle," Tom said without humour.

We went over the salary scale and our budget, looking for ways to help some of the people catch up to where they should be. Tom agreed we didn't want to be losing valuable people right now. That would send the wrong signal and make our recovery more difficult. I e-mailed him the salary schedule that Janice had conveniently formatted on Excel. It also showed the history of each individual's salary from five years previous. That would be helpful as well.

"I'm going to do something a little out of character, Tom," I said. "I'm going to team up with Michelle and start a program of calls on all the previous contacts we had in the architectural community as well as contractors. We want to get them comfortable with Trent once more and have them believing in us again."

"Boy, it didn't take you long to become a 'Trent Man,'" Tom chuckled. "But that's a really great plan, Dex. It's something I know you can do and with Michelle's help and contacts, I'm betting you'll surprise yourself at just how well you do. I'm all for that."

"Thanks. It's something proactive I can do instead of just sitting around the office all day. I just hope Michelle likes the idea too."

"You mean you haven't discussed it with her?"

"Not yet. Keep your fingers crossed. She's an important person in this company and I want to take advantage of her talents," I said.

"I'm not touching that line with a barge pole," Tom laughed.

By five o'clock that afternoon I was beat. Too much energy and tension had gone into the day. The enjoyment of giving the staff some hope for a better tomorrow had worn off in the afternoon as Janice and I worked to figure out just what to do about salaries.

She took it upon herself to draft an advertisement for a senior accountant and ran it by me that afternoon. I approved it and she said it would be in the Wednesday through Saturday editions of the morning and evening papers. I made a note to talk to Teresa Tremonte, our temporary head of accounting, first thing the next morning so that she was aware of what was going on. She would be invited to apply for the job if she chose.

The walk to the streetcar stop and the ride out Lakeshore Drive was a pleasant relief. A two-block walk to Michelle's apartment building was the completion of the journey. She had given me the keys to both the elevator-penthouse access and the door to the apartment before I left for work.

I was tired, but not down. I couldn't resist. "Honey, I'm home," I called as closed the door behind me.

I heard the strangled laugh from the kitchen then saw her broad smile as she came out to meet me.

"You just couldn't help yourself, could you?" she said as she wrapped her arms around my neck.

"Nope. You planted the seed on Friday so it's all your fault."

"How was your day?" she asked, changing the subject.

"It had its moments. I have been rewarded in my new position with several vexing problems, however."

"I guess that was to be expected. I'm sure some of them have been hanging around just waiting for the new boss to look after them," she smiled.

"Yes … that's very perceptive of you. Some of them are old problems. However, in talking to Tom this afternoon, he made it known that they are *my* problems now."

"Anything you can't solve?"

"I don't know yet. I have to find a new senior accountant. I have to find some money in the budget to reward staff for living through the salary freeze. And, I have to convince you that we should team up and start calling on all the old architect and contractor contacts that you and David made. Other than that, the rest is kid's stuff," I grinned.

"What's that last part again? You and me making calls?" she said warily.

"You got it, sweetie. You dress your sexiest and we'll take them to the University Club and get them wined and dined and we'll be back in business," I kidded.

"You're serious?"

"Yup. I may be making light of it but I'm told you and David were a very effective team in keeping our company name in front of the people who made decisions about which engineering firm to use on their projects. I'd like to re-establish that team approach."

She looked at me long and hard. I'm not sure what she was thinking but after a bit she broke into a smile.

"Alright," she said warily. "I want to see you work your magic on some of those crusty old buggers we had to put up with."

I pulled her into me again.

"Thank you. I was worried you might not want to. I'm not very confident about this myself, but I think we should take a stab at it."

"Maybe I've got more faith in you than you have. I think we might make a very effective team. You're nothing like David. Nowhere near as intense. I have a hunch you'll charm them much more easily than you think. You just be yourself and I'll be decoration."

"I'll have to rely on you to tell me who's who on the list of targets. You will have met most of them while I won't know any of them. I'm thinking we could do one or two each week if that's feasible," I suggested.

"I think that's very doable but we won't know until we try. When do you want me to start?" she asked with a smile.

"No time like the present. How about next week? You can cook up a list of contacts and we'll start making phone calls."

I was sitting, now. It was a large wing chair with an upright back, big enough for a very large person. On a small table beside me was a glass of single malt scotch, a brand I'd never heard of and, in the past, unlikely to have been able to afford. Michelle had finished the dinner preparations and was sitting across from me, waiting for the oven timer to signal our meal was ready.

I don't exactly know how I became aware of the change but I felt a tightness in my chest and it seemed to be intensifying. I put my head back in the chair and attempted to breathe slowly and relax every muscle I had control of. I couldn't seem to effect any change and the tightness continued to increase. Now I could feel the onset of a headache. This wasn't right.

"Michelle," I said weakly, looking toward her.

I remembered seeing the look of shock and then fear on her face before I lost consciousness.

Chapter 12
A Nasty Surprise

I awoke slowly, bits and pieces of consciousness coming and going along the way. I could hear sounds and when my brain collected enough information, I was fairly sure I was in a hospital. That made sense, although I had no idea why I was there. I tried to remember but all I could think of was the look on Michelle's face. I closed my eyes and let go of all thoughts once more.

My next moment of consciousness had a badly overweight nurse fussing over some machine that was beeping along quite happily on its own. Whatever happened to the lovely, lithe young ladies that used to populate the nursing corps? Once again, I drifted off.

I completely lost sense of time and place when I next awoke. I was no longer surprised to find myself in a hospital room, hooked up to various probes, tubes and other paraphernalia. I lay there for a while, now fully awake, wondering just what might have happened to me and when I would find out. A little judicious exploration revealed I had what I would learn later to be a nasal oxygen tube fitted around my head and a catheter in my penis.

My mind was functioning better now. I had a clue what had happened. I remembered the chest tightness and then blacking out. I guessed I had suffered a heart attack or something similar. A clock on the wall told me it was nearing seven o'clock but I had no idea whether it was am or pm. This time of year it would be light at either.

I closed my eyes and tried to think about what it might mean. A heart attack! As far as I knew, there was no history of heart problems in our family. I was a non-smoker and a light drinker since the fun of getting shit-faced evaporated sometime before I got married. I didn't weigh any more today than I did back in college. My time in the

Caribbean had corrected that. I exercised, although I had to admit it was pretty haphazard lately. What the hell had happened?

I must have dozed off again, waking when I felt a gentle touch on my arm and a soft voice calling me.

"Wake up, Mr. McLeod. Come on, time to wake up."

I opened my eyes to see the nurse I had observed before leaning over me with a smile and that oh-so-soothing voice.

"There you go. How are you feeling? Any pains or aches? Any discomfort?" she asked.

I shook my head a croaked a "no" in response.

"Water?" I gasped.

She passed me a foam cup with a bent straw and I sipped it greedily. I could feel the easing in my throat.

"Your doctor will be along shortly. He's probably going to want to ask you some questions. I'm sure he can tell you what's going on," she said sweetly.

If I had only heard her voice and not seen her, I would have pictured as a slim, lovely woman in her mid-twenties. No matter. She might not have been a picture of loveliness but she was reassuring and professional and I could live with that.

She moved around the room efficiently and made sure I was comfortable before she left. I could see what I assumed was an IV drip on a stand near my right side. I counted several electro-probes attached to my chest, neck and one arm. Wondering what they were recording I looked around. I could see a colour monitor showing a number of values, including heart rate, respiration and who knows what else. I was definitely wired for sound.

Twenty minutes later, a doctor walked into my room and introduced himself.

"Good morning, Mr. McLeod," he said in a friendly manner.

Well, that solved one mystery. It was morning. Just what day it was, I wasn't so sure.

"I'm Doctor Holtz. I'm a resident on the cardio ward and I'm going to be working with you for the time being."

"Good morning, doctor. Where am I?" I suddenly wondered.

"Lakeshore Regional Hospital. You were brought here when you had some sort of event at your home."

I nodded my understanding.

"What day is this?"

"It's Wednesday. They brought you in Monday night. We've been keeping an eye on you and making sure you're stable before we woke you up."

"Michelle? Where's Michelle?"

"Your wife had been here constantly since you arrived. I think she went home late last night to get some sleep. I didn't want to see her as a patient as well."

I didn't bother to correct him on our status.

"Any idea what happened?"

"I think we've got a pretty good idea but we'll need to do some scans and tests to confirm it. My gut tells me you have a wonky valve in your heart. Maybe more than one."

I kind of appreciated the humour the doctor chose in his description. He was making this sound something less than life-or-death.

"Fixable?"

"Easily. Probably with non-invasive surgery. That means we don't have to crack your chest open to repair it. Of course, that assumes our guess is correct. We'll know better later today. Why don't I get a little history on you?" he smiled.

For the next fifteen minutes he asked questions and I answered them to the best of my ability. I could see him nodding and occasionally smiling.

"Well, your history and habits indicate just what we think might be the problem. You may have been carrying this around with you for quite some time and be completely unaware of it. I'd like to know what brought it on, though."

I shook my head and shrugged. I had no idea.

"Have you been under stress lately? Home life, job, that sort of thing."

"Job, I guess. I'm a newly appointed general manager at a local firm. It's a whole new thing for me. Something I'd never been trained for and never thought I'd achieve."

"Ah, well that could be a contributor, all right."

"I'm in the final stages of getting a divorce, as well."

"Another factor that could add to your stress. Anything else?"

"No ... not really."

"Good. Well, we're going to put you through some scans and tests today so be prepared to be run around the hospital a couple of times. I'll see you again tomorrow morning when we have a better idea of what might be wrong with you."

"Thank you. When can I see Michelle ... my wife," I added quickly.

"As soon as she returns. I'll let the duty nurse know it's okay."

Michelle showed up a little after ten. I didn't think it was possible for her to look haggard but she did this morning. I could see her eyes were red and bloodshot and her jaw was trembling as she approached my bed.

"Dex? Are you all right?" Her voice was tentative and uncertain. She was clearly very upset.

"I'm going to be fine," I reassured her. That might have been premature but she didn't need any more doubt.

I raised my hand, mindful of the tubes and took hers, squeezing it in confirmation.

"Oh, Dex. I was so scared. I thought I might lose you. I couldn't go through that again. I just couldn't."

"I know, love. Don't you worry about me. The doctor was in earlier and they think they know what's wrong and it's something they can easily fix."

"Are you sure?"

"As sure as I can be. They're going to do a bunch of tests today and then they'll know for sure. Don't go worrying yourself sick now. You look like you've been having a bad time and I don't want to see that."

She nodded with a grimace that was an attempt at a smile. She bent over and kissed me. A nice, long, sensitive kiss that left me feeling a lot better. I hope it did the same for her.

"Do Rueben and Tom know what happened?"

She nodded again. "Yes, I called them yesterday morning before I knew you were still unconscious. The hospital told me you were in intensive care and stable. They didn't know any more than that."

"I woke up just this morning. I guess they wanted me quiet for a while until they could figure out what happened. Have you had any sleep in the last day or so?"

"Not much. A little early this morning. I couldn't get my mind to shut off. I kept thinking about what happened to David and now you. I couldn't believe it was happening all over again."

"It isn't. I'm still here and it wasn't an aneurism. They think it might be a heart valve. If it is, it's no big deal to fix it."

"Oh, I hope so, dear. I need you so much. I love you, Dex. I truly, truly, love you."

"Do you? God, that sounds good. I love you too, Michelle. I don't think I realized it until you weren't here when I woke up. I wasn't afraid for my health, I was afraid I might not see you."

Now the tears came. I had to assume they were happy tears because she was kissing me and holding me by the shoulders, all the while blubbering like a baby. I felt nothing but relief. I was alive and I was in love and I finally admitted it to myself. Thoughts of Sandra never once entered my mind. There was no comparison between Michelle and my ex-wife. For all her status and wealth, Michelle was a giving person. I was sure now that she was the right one for me.

Thursday morning and Michelle was once more by my side. She looked so much better today than she did yesterday. She would be with me when Dr. Holtz gave me the results of the tests; good or bad. She insisted and I wouldn't deny her. Not if she was really going to act like my wife.

When I was admitted, Michelle gave them all the necessary information that she could glean from my wallet. Since we were living at the same address, the admitting staff assumed we were married. A lucky break for both of us. If I had my way, we would be confirming that properly sometime in the near future.

Dr. Holtz explained that his suspicion had been confirmed and that one of the valves in my heart had a malformation that probably occurred before I was born. I had carried this defect around with me for nearly fifty years without any hint of a problem until now. Happily, it could be corrected with non-invasive surgery, and he recommended that I be scheduled for that as soon as possible. Neither Michelle nor I were about to argue with him.

"As soon as possible" turned out to be five weeks, the second week of September. I had been resting at home for most of it, with supervised visits to the office with Michelle making sure I didn't get too involved in the day-to-day. I was pleased that the office was doing well under Reuben's supervision but everyone wished me a speedy return. Our trip to the French Riviera had been postponed.

I was admitted the day before the surgery was scheduled, and the next thing I knew I was being wheeled out of the operating theatre and back to my room. An hour later, Dr. Holtz stopped by to let me know the surgeon had said everything went exactly according to plan and I should be as good as new in a couple of days.

Three days later I was on my way back to the apartment with Michelle. I had been told to take it easy and not get involved in any strenuous exercise for two weeks. I would then be back to see my doctor for a follow-up. Michelle floored me when she asked the doctor about sex. He smiled and said it would be fine as long as we didn't get too carried away. I wasn't sure about what "too carried away" meant but I didn't think I would test the boundaries.

My realization that I loved Michelle wasn't some bolt-from-the-blue revelation. It snuck up on me when I first awoke in the hospital that morning after my collapse. I was disappointed that I didn't see her there. That stuck with me for the rest of the time before she arrived and then I knew what it meant. I wanted her there. I wanted her to be with me. There wasn't anyone else. Her reaction to my condition was all the proof I needed that she felt the same way. I didn't need her to tell me she loved me. It was her actions, not her words that told the tale.

We didn't make love that first few days. I think Michelle was being overly protective of me. But in bed at night she held me to her and rained soft kisses on me. It was great medicine and I returned them, getting a bit bolder with them each day. At last, five days after I had been released, we joined. I didn't last very long at first but with a little help from her, I managed a second session that was much more satisfying for her. There were no after effects from the effort except euphoria.

"Now that I'm getting my strength back, I'm going to be able to bend you over the kitchen counter and have my way with you again," I chuckled.

"Promises, promises," she laughed. "I'm just so happy you're better and we don't have to worry about it happening again. The doctor said everything else is fine and you're in very good health. It's probably what kept you from having this happen even sooner."

"Moving on to another subject," I began. "Michelle, you know I love you. It took me a while to realize it but I do. Will you marry me?"

She looked at me in surprise, but quickly recovered.

"Yes. I will. I will marry you," she cried, tears now flowing freely. She wrapped her arms around my neck and held me closely.

It took a while before she regained her composure and then kissed me, thoroughly and deeply.

"I think we should go looking for a ring today," I suggested.

"No. No, we won't," she said, holding up her left hand. "This ring was my grandmother's and was given to me by her. I promised to wear it for the rest of my life. I don't want you to think it's a symbol of David. It's a family heirloom, and I hope you understand that."

"Yes ... of course. It's a very beautiful ring and I'm happy you want to respect your grandmother's memory. But I would like to get you something that symbolizes our engagement and love. What do you suggest?"

"Your body in my bed every night and waking up to see you every morning," she smiled.

"Very nice, but not quite what I had in mind. Something more tangible. Maybe a tattoo or a piercing?" I kidded.

"Never!" she spat. "Not in a million years!" she reemphasized.

"Okay ... let's see ...," I began again.

"Don't bother. Teasing me won't help you find the answer. I'm going to give you a few days to think of something and you'd better be serious about it. Just as serious about it as you are about me."

I didn't get the impression she was kidding so I nodded acceptance of her condition.

I know Michelle contacted her family to let them know she intended to remarry. I heard a couple of the conversations in the evening but she was reluctant to discuss them with me. In any event, she assured me that all of her living family, mother included, would be invited to the wedding.

I would contact my parents and offspring to let them know as well. It had been over two years since Sandra and I had separated. I wondered what their reaction would be. I wasn't worried about my parents. They didn't particularly warm to Sandra in the first place, although I never really knew why. We weren't estranged but my father had taken an early retirement and they travelled quite a bit. I envied them and hoped that within a few years, Michelle and I could emulate them.

~~***~~

Michelle and I initiated our program of visits to architects and contractors the following week. We decided we would re-visit those whom she and David had formerly made contact with. It turned out to be a good decision. In each case, they remembered Michelle and welcomed her visit. It was our first one that caused me concern. I wasn't sure just what to expect and I hoped I wouldn't be found wanting.

"Hello, Mr. Whitmore," Michelle said brightly as we were welcomed by one of the senior partners of McAllister, Fulton, and Whitmore, Architects.

"Please, Michelle, I thought we had progressed to 'Charles' when last we met," he smiled.

"Thank you, Charles. I'd like to introduce Dexter McLeod, our General Manager. There's been reorganization at Trent Engineering and I thought you might want to hear about it."

Michelle was smooth and we were welcomed and escorted into a meeting room. She gave a brief synopsis of what had changed at Trent in the last year and suggested I had been the driving force behind those changes. Whitmore turned to me and gave me a questioning look.

"I don't recall you from my previous visit to Trent, Mr. McLeod."

"No, sir. I'm from Vancouver and I've only been here in Toronto a few months. I have been at Pinecone Engineering for over twenty years, however."

"And what is your area of expertise?" he asked, clearly curious.

I was caught with a question I didn't expect, so I answered truthfully.

"Design. My skills are related to converting concepts to finished designs via computer."

"Well, that's certainly an important area in any business. Keeping up with all the changes is a bit overwhelming, I imagine. Everything I read suggests the ground moves on a regular and frequent basis," he grinned.

I breathed a silent sigh of relief. I had passed the first test.

"Dex has re-made our design department, Charles," Michelle slipped in. "We would be delighted if you and any of your staff would care to visit the offices at any time in the future. I think you'll be quite impressed with the new vitality at Trent."

"I'd like to, Michelle. Perhaps we can have lunch one day and a tour."

"The University Club suit you?"

"That would be very nice. I'll have my secretary check my schedule and I'll let you know when we can find some time."

The meeting ended a few minutes later and Michelle and I left the offices, my chest still tight from tension. It had gone much better than I expected, particularly since I had fielded the unexpected question about my "expertise."

As we stepped out onto the sidewalk, I breathed another sigh of relief, this time audibly.

"You were great, Dex," Michelle smiled and hugged my arm. "Your answer to his question was just right. Well done."

I nodded in agreement. "That was something I didn't expect but I gather from his comments it's an area that interests him so I'll make sure we have a good show for him when he visits. For a first time, I thought we did okay."

"We did very well, thanks to you," she said. "Our next one should be easier. Charles isn't the most outgoing man and I thought our reception today was much better than I anticipated. Here's hoping they all go as well as that."

Over the next month we visited two other architectural firms and four general contractors. I quickly discovered I was much more at ease with the contractors than with the architects. My field experience and my opinions on how the relationship should be between general contractors and engineering firms was in parallel with their beliefs and that made our conversations much more free-flowing and informative.

I was sure it would be several months before we saw any fruit from our visits but I was wrong. I had a call from Charles Whitmore inviting us to bid on a new project less than two weeks after our visit and before he had made his social call on our office. A week later, a general contractor asked us to intervene on their behalf in a dispute with a steel fabrication sub-trade related to the interpretation of specifications. This was a dangerous situation. We didn't need to make enemies either of the general contactor or the sub.

Rueben and I visited the site and listened to both sides of the argument. I knew I wasn't qualified to make a judgment but Rueben took that worry away. Within a few minutes of looking at the specifications and plans, he suggested a compromise that seemed to satisfy both parties. No hard feelings and both the contractor and fabricator thanked us for our help.

"I like the way you guys think," Gus Molinari said as we headed off toward our vehicles. "We can work with people like you, Dex ... Rueben. I'll let my people know just how much you helped solve that problem. Thanks again," he said, holding out his hand.

We shook and parted, heading back to the office.

"Well done, Rueben. I was worried it was going to become a pissing match to see who would win. You defused that perfectly."

"Thanks. I don't think they could have come up with that solution without an engineer to approve it. They needed us and I think Gus saw that right away. The fabricator didn't but he was grateful it didn't cost him an arm and a leg to fix the problem."

"Well, someone told them to contact us so I guess Michelle's and my visits are beginning to show results."

"Yeah. Just what we needed too. I've got a good feeling about what's happening at Trent, Dex. I can feel the energy and I haven't felt that for some time. Anytime you need me or one of my people to help on this type of problem, don't think twice about asking. It will pay dividends, I'm sure of it."

"I think so too," I agreed.

~~***~~

The wedding had been set for the third Saturday in October. The invitations had been sent and the replies were coming in. My parents said they would attend and planned to be in Toronto the week before the event. I didn't know their friends that they would be staying with. I was very happy they were making the effort.

I purchased an airline ticket for Meredith to come as well once she had indicated she wanted to attend. Michelle insisted that she stay with us in the apartment rather than a hotel and to tell the truth, I was delighted that she did. Jon sent his regrets but wished us all the best and arranged for a gift to be delivered before the ceremony. It was a case of a very fine vintage Chilean Cabernet.

It was Michelle's side of the family that seemed to be slow responding. She didn't seem to be upset about it so I didn't express any concern but I did find it odd. The first to confirm would attend was her brother, Mark, in Montreal, then son Kyle and father William, or Billy as he preferred to be called. We had heard nothing from Michelle's mother, Martha, or her older son and her older brother.

We had already conducted two tours of the office for prospective clients and they were very well received. Charles Whitmore brought his junior partner along who turned out to be a computer "geek." He had more than a dozen questions about the CADD systems we employed and what I saw on the horizon. He was also interested in whether we could "model" some of their designs for them for presentation purposes. It would be a lot cheaper than conventional modeling.

Our second tour was for Humber Contracting, the firm that we had helped in the dispute with the steel fabricator. That visit was primarily held in the engineering section as they got into discussions of design and practical application. Gus Molinari and I chatted about my project in Sint Maarten. His company was looking for foreign work and wondered what the problems might be. We agreed to consult with him if we had some useful experience.

I was sitting in my office the next day when I had a phone call.

"Mr. McLeod, my name is Michael Catchpole. I am Michelle's older brother. I think we should meet for lunch this week. I believe we need to talk."

I didn't warm to his voice. His tone said he wasn't making a request as such; he was giving me an order. I almost told him that I wasn't available this week but changed my mind when I remembered this was Michelle's family.

"I think I can find the time. Would the University Club suit you," I said, trying to push back at some of his implied arrogance.

"That will do fine. Tomorrow then?" he asked, trying to force the issue.

"Let's make it Thursday instead, Mr. Catchpole. I have guests in the office tomorrow." I didn't really but I couldn't resist pushing back at him.

"Very well," he said with a note of reluctant acceptance. "Thursday at noon, then."

If I'd have written down the conversation verbatim, it wouldn't have looked anywhere near as rude as his tone of voice made it sound. Worse, he had pushed me into being less than polite as well. Ah well, I'll know what to expect from him after I talk to Michelle.

"He's his mother's son," Michelle said as we sat in the living room before supper. "He's convinced he's someone important and likes to lord it over anyone he meets. It doesn't always work. It certainly doesn't work on me or his father. You have my permission to give as good as you get."

"Well, I haven't heard what he has to say, but his tone is pretty aggressive."

"He wants to see who has the audacity to marry his sister without getting his permission. After all, he is the elder brother," she smirked.

"Ah ... so ... the western upstart offends the western pretender," I laughed.

"Something like that. I can't see Michael in Calgary, to be honest. He'd be much better in Ottawa or even England with his attitude. By the way, don't call him Mike. He hates that."

"So I guess I shouldn't be looking for someone with a ten gallon hat and big silver belt buckle, huh?"

"No ... more like a charcoal suit, dark tie and starched white shirt with cufflinks. I wouldn't be surprised if his underwear wasn't starched," she snorted.

"It's going to be an interesting meeting. I'll do my best not to offend him and I'll try to get him to come to the wedding if he hasn't already decided to."

"Good luck," Michelle grinned as she rose to go to the kitchen and serve our meal.

I was physically and mentally prepared for my meeting with Michael Catchpole. I had chosen a dark blue suit, white dress shirt and dark burgundy tie. I was as "eastern" as I could get with my wardrobe. Michelle approved. Mentally, her support of my not having to accept his condescension or insults gave me the freedom to respond as I saw fit.

In the end, I wanted him to at least acknowledge that Michelle had the right to choose whomever she wanted for a partner. I also wanted him to attend the wedding and not upset his only sister. I wasn't sure what the outcome would be, so I would just have to "play it by ear."

I was five minutes early at the University Club and the maitre d' seated me immediately. It was almost fifteen minutes later that I saw him lead another man toward my table. I rose as he approached.

"Hello, I'm Dexter McLeod," I said politely with what I hoped was a sincere smile and an extended hand.

"Michael Catchpole," he replied unsmiling. His handshake was weak and brief.

He seated himself and I followed. He was an inch or two shorter than me and very slim. He had a hawk-like face that was clean-shaven and unremarkable other than his penetrating blue eyes and prominent nose. His hair was cut professionally short and was almost completely grey. As Michelle had predicted, he was wearing a charcoal suit, white shirt, and dark blue and red striped tie.

I was wondering how I would get a conversation started. I had almost forgotten that it was he who had asked for the meeting.

"I thought it appropriate to meet the man who intends to marry my sister," he announced. "I'm surprised and disappointed that I hadn't heard anything about you from her before receiving the invitation to the wedding."

"Do you talk to Michelle often?" I asked, knowing full well he didn't.

"No ... not often. We don't have much in common, it seems."

"You're both family," I stated the obvious.

"There are times...," he began, then stopped. "Our family isn't very close as you probably already know, Mr. McLeod."

"Call me Dex, please Michael. I'd feel more comfortable if you did."

He looked at me for a moment before responding.

"Very well, Dex. Tell me how you met my sister."

I recited the short version of her contacting me and our brief relationship, leading to where we were today.

"I gather she's very impressed with your accomplishments at Trent. I wouldn't have expected that," he said.

"Why?"

"Trent is an old firm and had lived on the good graces of the Toronto establishment for many years. For you to come in and try and recover from the loss of that connection was, to say the least, presumptuous."

Somewhere in his voice, I detected just the slightest hint of admiration.

"Sometimes, when you don't know any better, you just plunge in and do what you think is right," I said. "Perhaps ... just perhaps, the old Toronto establishment isn't as well established as it used to be."

I think my answer caught him by surprise. For moment he said nothing, remaining expressionless. Then, against all odds, I saw the beginning of a smile.

"My time in Calgary has taught me that not everyone in the business community bows to the east. My best wishes on your efforts. I'm surprised but perhaps I shouldn't be. I've always respected Michelle's judgment and in your case, that seems to be proven once again. My congratulations on your engagement as well," he said, holding his hand out once more.

This time his grip was firm and warm. Whatever ice had been present earlier at our meeting had been melted and I sensed we were going to get along well.

"Thank you. I feel very lucky that she has accepted me. Can I assume you and your wife will attend the wedding?"

"Yes, of course. I will let Michelle know that her son Carter will also be there."

"Great ... I'm really pleased to hear that."

"Have you heard from mother yet?"

"No. Unfortunately we haven't."

"I'll call her and see if I can't get her answer promptly. I assume my father has responded positively?"

"Yes, he has, as has your brother, Mark, and nephew Kyle."

"What about your family, Dex?"

"My daughter Meredith and my parents will be here. My son is in Chile and can't get away. He sent a gift however."

We ordered our meal and chatted about inconsequential things for the rest of the lunch. I was warming to Michael. He wasn't quite the "stuffed shirt" I was led to believe. I wondered what ... or who ... had changed him.

"You aren't what I expected," I finally said in a moment of candour.

"Ah ... well ... I suppose I can guess what you were told. Uptight, formal, old school type with no sense of humour. That about it?"

"Ha Ha," I chuckled. "Pretty close. But you dress the part."

"I'm in Toronto. This club has certain expectations. Now, if we were in Calgary, that would be quite a different matter."

"How so?"

"Well, no charcoal suit unless I was going before the Board of Directors. More likely a sport coat or blazer, slacks, open-neck shirt, loafers. I had to buy this shirt just for our meeting," he grinned.

"Sounds a lot like our Vancouver office. So … I've been misled about you then."

"Well, let's just say I had an epiphany when I arrived in Calgary. Discovering that Toronto wasn't the centre of the universe and that the economy was largely resource based put quite a different light on matters. I had to change my perspective somewhat."

"I'm going through that in reverse, I think. But with Michelle's guidance, I'm doing better at appealing to the *Upper Canadian* business sensibilities."

He raised his water glass in salute. "Good luck to you, Dex. I think your idea of including Michelle in your plans is excellent."

"Thank you … but where do you get all this information about us from?"

"Why from the only reliable source at Trent of course, Janice Meriwether," he grinned again.

"I might have known. Well, that just shows who really runs Trent Engineering."

"I never realized just how important someone like Janice was until I had my own office to run," Michael admitted. "My 'Janice' is named Lorna, and she's invaluable. She also conspires with my wife to make sure I don't forget important dates or events. I couldn't do without her."

By the time we'd finished our coffee and had run out of conversation, I had a completely different picture of Michael Catchpole. He wasn't who he was portrayed to be and I wondered if even Michelle knew that. I would be interested in her reaction to my meeting.

Chapter 13
Meet the Family

When I arrived home Thursday evening after my lunch with Michael, Michelle was anxious to hear how it went.

"I think you've been deceiving me, love," I began. "Your brother is nothing like you described him. We had a delightful lunch and got along very well. He congratulated me on our engagement and assured me he would be at the wedding with his wife and your son. On top of that, he will call your mother and insist she attend as well. So ... now what do you have to say?" I said with a questioning grin.

Michelle was dumbstruck by my synopsis. She looked at me as if she didn't believe what I was telling her.

"Are you serious? Michael was nice ... and polite ... and friendly?"

"Absolutely! You obviously don't know your brother as well as you think you do. Maybe you should give him a call before he calls you. I suggested you and your family didn't communicate very frequently and he agreed."

"Where is he staying?"

"At the Hyatt. Call him," I suggested a little more firmly.

She did. Dinner was late that evening. They were on the phone for over an hour. When she finally hung up, she came over to me, her eyes red and tear tracks on her cheeks. She plopped herself in my lap and planted a most loving kiss on me.

"You are amazing," she whispered when the lip-lock finished. "Michael barely tolerated David. But you ... he thinks you're just the right guy for me. Good thing we agree, huh?"

"I never had a moment's doubt," I lied.

~~***~~

Friday came and went and we might have had the weekend to ourselves but at the last minute I decided to see if I could contact Michelle's mother. A pre-emptive strike as it were. Bad idea.

"What do you want, Mr. McLeod? Are you looking for my approval of this ridiculous marriage? Well ... that's not going to happen. You two barely know each other and I doubt you are the kind of person that is capable of giving my daughter the lifestyle she is accustomed to. My son seems to think you are a good choice but I can hardly see why. You don't come from a prominent family and you aren't from this part of the country. As far as I'm concerned, she's about to make another predictable mistake."

"Well, I'm sorry you feel that way about me, Mrs. Catchpole. Nevertheless, I hope for Michelle's sake that you will attend the wedding. I know she and Michael and Martin would want you there."

"I very much doubt I will attend. I'm very annoyed with my daughter. She has never even presented you to me for my approval."

"That's probably my fault, Mrs. Catchpole. I should have insisted that I meet you before ... and I didn't."

"It was my daughter's responsibility, not yours," she snapped. "There are social rules about these sorts of things and Michelle has yet to learn to respect them."

I could hear the "Oxbridge" accent clearly as her forcefulness increased. She was back living in the "old country" and playing by a set of norms that didn't exist here in Canada.

"Well ... I'll leave it to your best judgment about attending. I hope for Michelle's sake that you choose to come. Thank you for listening to me," I finished. The next sound was the click of her hanging up the telephone.

I walked back to the living room and flopped in the chair I had become accustomed to as mine.

There was a slight smile on Michelle's face as she saw my frown and wrinkled brow.

"You can't win them all, Dex."

"No ... I guess not. I had hoped that Michael would have convinced her but it doesn't sound like it. You don't seem too broken-hearted about it."

"I'm not. She can be a real ... witch ... when she wants to be. You must meet my father. You'll understand quickly enough why they couldn't co-exist. In fact, if you'd like to, why don't we drive down to Amherstburg this weekend. I'm sure they'll put us up in Dad's home on Lake Erie."

"Okay, I'd like that. But don't you think we should call first to let him know we're coming?"

"Yes ... I'll look after that. You will love him. I know it. I should have done this sooner."

Her phone call was brief and she returned to the living room with a big smile.

"He's delighted we're coming and can't wait to meet you. We can have a nice afternoon and Sunday morning with them."

"Great," I smiled.

"It's about a three-and-a-half-hour drive, so we'll need to get an early start," she warned.

"It looks like we'll have nice weather, and I haven't been out of the city since I arrived months ago. I'm looking forward to the visit."

"Good. I know you'll like Dad. He's such a down-to-earth kind of guy."

With some guidance from Michelle, we arrived at her father's home just before noon. We hadn't been in any rush and the weekend traffic was light on the 401. The house was more of a cottage that had been updated and expanded, but it was right on the beach and had an unrestricted view to the south.

As we pulled into the narrow crushed rock driveway, the front door opened and two people appeared. The man … William, I assumed, was lean and angular looking, with a full head of grey hair and wearing a t-shirt and jeans. The woman was somewhat younger I thought, and definitely more rounded. Both of them wore big smiles as we climbed out of the car.

"Hello!" William called as he approached. "How are you Michelle?" He was wearing a mile-wide smile as he wrapped his arms around his daughter.

"You must be Dex," he said, releasing Michelle and extending his hand, still showing his big smile.

"I am. Nice to meet you, Sir."

"Oh, please, it's Billy to my friends and several of my enemies," he laughed.

He turned toward the woman and took her hand.

"This is Carolyn, the love of my life. Carolyn, this is Dexter McLeod, Michelle's fiancé."

"Lovely to meet you, Dexter. I'm so happy Michelle has found someone. Congratulations," she beamed, hugging me in place of a handshake.

"Thank you ... and it's Dex to my friends."

As the introductions were going on, I saw Michelle standing to one side and grinning at the effusive greeting from her father and his lady. I had the feeling it was going to be quite a pleasant stay in their home.

We followed them inside and Billy immediately produced a beer, handing it to me in the bottle. Carolyn passed Michelle a glass of white wine and we all toasted each other. It was completely casual and natural that I immediately felt at home with them. There wasn't a hint of pretension or cautiousness from either of them.

"We're having a few friends over for a barbeque this evening so Carolyn made lunch. We'll probably be eating a little later so don't hesitate to dig in," Billy said.

"You couldn't resist, could you Dad? Any reason for a celebration will do, eh?" Michelle laughed.

"You know me well, girl. I may be old but not so old that I don't enjoy a good time with good people."

"You aren't old, Dad," Michelle chided. "Why you're not even seventy yet. You're in good health and good spirits; so don't give me that 'old' stuff. Am I right, Carolyn?"

"You know it, kid. He's got lots of life in him yet ... trust me," she giggled.

I was watching the happy byplay of the three and got the distinct impression that there was a lot of love going on between them. Carolyn and Michelle acted a lot like co-conspirators, trading secrets between each other. Billy looked genuinely happy and satisfied with his life. What more would any man want?

Carolyn brought out a tray of sandwiches and a bowl of potato chips, while Billy returned with a bottle of white wine for the ladies and two more beers for us. We sat on the front porch overlooking the lake for a while until it got too hot and we moved to the back deck where the barbeque would be held. Even though it was September, the weather was pleasantly warm.

The guests began arriving just after four in the afternoon and by the time the first three groups had been introduced; I knew I had no hope of remembering all the names. By five-thirty there must have been over twenty people on the deck, all of them familiar with each other. The ages ranged from early forties to late seventies, I guessed. But everyone seemed to enjoy each other's company. I had a number of conversations about a wide range of topics from living on the west coast to my time in the Caribbean.

There was no common thread among the guests save the fact that they were all neighbours and/or friends of Billy and Carolyn. Their backgrounds were just as diverse: a lawyer, two auto plant workers, a newspaperman, a women's wear shop owner, more than a couple of retired people and so on. An eclectic group that all seemed to be happy in each other's company. Billy and Carolyn were well endowed with friends.

"I don't think I've enjoyed anything quite as much as this since our picnic at Zarek's farm," I told Michelle.

"Dad is that kind of person, Dex. He attracts friends like some people collect stamps. Can you imagine how confined he must have felt married to my mother? This has all happened since they divorced. He's happier here than I can ever remember him at home."

"I like Carolyn a lot, too," I said. "She's seems exactly right for him."

"Yes. I feel the same way. She's ten years younger, but I think she keeps Dad young. Anyway, she's happy, he's happy, so I'm happy."

"Will they ever marry?"

"No … not according to them. They don't think it's necessary. It's just a legal complication and not at all important to either of them."

"What's the legal complication?"

"Carolyn's husband took off on her twenty years ago. At the time, she couldn't afford a divorce so she was just abandoned. As far as they know, her husband is still alive. Arnold, I think she said his name was. Anyway, there hasn't been any need to spend the money on a lawyer and there's no sign he's coming back, so they just live together as if they were married. According to their lawyer friend over there," she said, pointing at one of the guests, "she can bide her time without any negative consequences."

"I suppose we could do the same thing," I said, looking slyly at Michelle as I offered the opinion.

She looked back at me with a serious expression. "I suppose we could. Is that what you want?"

I pulled her to me and kissed her fully in front of everyone who might have been watching.

"What do you think?"

She smiled and I could feel her relax again. We remained with our arms around each other.

Every one of the guests had brought something to the event and there was more food than could possibly have been eaten. I favoured the hickory smoked baby back ribs, coleslaw and sour cream potato salad for my meal. I also tried one of the venison sausages that a guest had provided. They were outstanding and it was a shame they weren't available commercially. He had made them himself after a successful hunt somewhere up north.

The party broke up as guests began wandering off shortly after ten and the last leaving before midnight. It had been a wonderful afternoon and evening and I had met a number of very interesting people.

"That was a very fine party, Carolyn … Billy. I really like your friends. You are fortunate to have so many that enjoy being with you. Everyone brought something as well."

"We have these about once every two or three weeks," Carolyn said. "Some are here and some at other houses in the area. We're very lucky to have so many nice people as neighbors. I credit Billy for that. He's such a good neighbour and is always ready to help anyone who needs it. He's become the local handyman."

She smiled up at him, holding him around the waist and kissing him in appreciation. He was beaming at her compliment. They looked like a very happy couple and I couldn't help thinking that I wanted that kind of relationship with Michelle. I also couldn't help thinking that if I was asked to name my personal friends outside of work, it would be a short list. I was a loner, it seemed. Perhaps that was my nature or perhaps circumstances had made it so.

Michelle must have picked up on my thoughts because she turned to me.

"Dex … you never talk about your friends."

I looked at her and couldn't help telling her the truth.

"I don't really have any outside of work and a couple of people I've met since my divorce."

"It's something you have to work at," Billy offered. "Michelle's mother was … is … like that as well. She's happy to be on her own. I don't think she missed me for ten seconds," he said without malice. "I didn't know what friends were until I moved here to stay with a friend after my divorce. He got me out and had me meeting the locals and one thing led to another. I met Carolyn that way, thank God."

"I'll bet Michelle can get you doing the same thing, Dex," Carolyn offered. "Didn't you say you were calling on customers or something?"

"Yes … we are … and much to my surprise," I said, "I'm enjoying it. I was pretty nervous at first, but once I got used to it I found I liked meeting new people and talking about our business. In fact, I'm not sure I don't talk too much," I chuckled.

"You're doing just fine, dear," Michelle smiled. "I'm getting as much out of it as you are. It's good to have something important to do with your husband … or husband-to-be."

"You know, if you'd planned an earlier wedding, I would have suggested you have it on the beach or in that nice park near your apartment," Billy said. "We don't need big, fancy weddings at our age. A civil ceremony and big party are just the ticket."

I looked at Michelle and I could almost hear the wheels turning.

"Is it too late?" I asked.

"Well, we would have to contact all the people who've responded but that's not that many," she said thoughtfully. "The park has a big covered area in case it rained and we could rent some of those propane heaters on stands the restaurants use. Should we see if it's possible?" she asked.

I think she was looking for a yes from me, so I wasn't going to disappoint her.

"Let's do it. What do you think, Carolyn … Billy?"

"I think you're beginning to catch on, Dex," Billy grinned. "Life is about having the best time you can with the time you've got left. I think it would be a hoot. You might want to suggest casual dress too. The more comfortable people are, the more they will enjoy the experience. It will be something different for them … that's for sure."

"It's settled then," Michelle said. "Assuming we can rent the facility, we'll go ahead and set it all up."

We retired soon afterwards, lying in each other's arms, warmed in the afterglow of a wonderful afternoon and evening with Michelle's father, Carolyn, and their friends. I got the impression that Michelle would have been happy if Carolyn were her actual mother as they seemed to be very compatible together.

I slept well and when I awoke at my usual six o'clock it was still dark. Michelle rolled towards me and held me to her. I didn't want to wake her but a few moments later, I felt her hand move down toward my groin and carefully hold my cock. It was only seconds before I became erect and her hand began slowly stroking me.

"I missed out on this last night," she mumbled. "I heard Dad and Carolyn, but you were asleep already."

"I'm awake now," I said, slipping my hand up under her sleeveless t-shirt. I ran my thumb over a nipple and heard her moan in response. I pulled her on top of me and pushed her panties down as far as my hands would reach. She kicked them off, spread her legs, and reached back to grasp me once more and guide me into her. She was wet in anticipation and I slipped into her with little resistance.

"Hmmmm …," she groaned in satisfaction as I began to slowly move my hips and thrust into her. "That's nice … just like that."

It was like being on sexual cruise control. You got the feeling that you didn't have to do anything but maintain the rhythm and it could go on forever. I don't know how long it did last but some light was beginning to show through the blinds when I knew I wasn't going to be able to carry on any longer.

"I'm going to finish now," I whispered into her ear.

"Yes … please. It was so good. What a wonderful way to start the day."

"I agree. Puts you in a good mood, that's for sure."

We showered together before I left the bathroom to Michelle. I could hear some activity in the kitchen, so I was pretty sure we weren't the only ones up.

We walked into the kitchen together and found Carolyn making a breakfast for us. She turned away from the stove and walked to Michelle, giving her a big hug and then repeated the gesture with me.

"Good morning," she smiled at us. "I'm very happy you're here. Billy is so pleased you took the trouble to drive all the way down here to introduce Dex. We both think you make a lovely couple."

I guessed Carolyn's age to be somewhere between Michelle's and Billy's. Perhaps sixty but a very well preserved sixty. She obviously spent a good deal of time outdoors by the look of her tan and she appeared to be very fit.

"Thank you Carolyn," I said. "You've made us feel very welcome and it was a delight to meet your friends yesterday. We had a great time."

"Billy will be back in a couple of minutes. He's just walked down to the store to get the Sunday paper. He couldn't live without it," she laughed.

"Can I help?" Michelle asked, looking over Carolyn's shoulder.

"I'm almost done, dear. Maybe you can set the table for me, please."

Michelle was almost finished when I heard the front door open and Billy appeared with the big Sunday edition in his hands.

"Good morning folks. I trust you slept well," he smiled.

"Very well," I said, returning his smile.

"Breakfast is ready," Carolyn announced. "Wash your hands, Billy. You know how that paper leaves ink on them."

Michelle's father disappeared into the bathroom and returned a moment later as we all sat.

"We don't usually have a big breakfast like this but since this is a special occasion," Carolyn said, leaving the statement unfinished.

Michelle and I had not been accustomed to big breakfasts either but we indulged our hostess and host and made no apology for our gluttony. In the back of my mind I decided this would easily last us until suppertime, a reasonable assumption I felt. Michelle didn't make it as far as I did but gave it a game try.

We sat on the front porch, drank coffee, and talked, whiling away most of the morning until it was time for us to return to the city. I was beginning to regret having that big breakfast now as I was feeling a bit lethargic. I fortified myself with a large cup of black coffee before we parted and hoped it would last me until we were home.

As it turned out, I had to make a pit stop for gas just before Woodstock and I took the opportunity to empty my bladder and then fuel myself with another coffee. Michelle had warned me about the traffic heading back toward the city on a Sunday afternoon, even this late in the year. She was right. Just after Kitchener, we slowed to a steady crawl and it was well after five before we were back in the apartment. Luckily for Michelle, she had slept a good portion of the trip and had some energy left when we arrived.

She made a light meal for us and we talked about how much we enjoyed the weekend with Billy.

"It seems so odd that your father could have married your mother when his personality is so completely different," I said.

"He wasn't always like that, Dex. He was a pretty normal dad, going to work and coming home, cutting the lawn and doing odd jobs around the house. But mother was never satisfied with him. His job wasn't good enough, the house wasn't big enough, the car wasn't new enough. She just picked at him relentlessly, especially as we got older. He told me once it was like being bitten to death by a duck," she grimaced.

"Yeah, I can see where that would grind on him all right. But he's nothing like that now. I don't think I've ever met anyone whom I liked quite as quickly as him. He has an infectious way about him that you can't resist."

"Well, my mother managed to resist it," she growled. Then she looked at me thoughtfully. "You know, Dex, I think you might be a bit like my father. You told me that you were … what … socially withdrawn … not outgoing … not too many friends?"

I nodded, "Yes, but I don't think I could be compared to your father – at least not as I view him."

"I wasn't thinking of it that way but you aren't like the man you were describing any more either. You are more outgoing and you do enjoy the company of other people. I've watched you as we've held our meetings with the architects and contractors and you've looked at ease and handled yourself very well. I think it was just a matter of allowing yourself to be more social.

"I have a feeling those two women in Sint Maarten had a lot to do with that. You came to Toronto with nothing more than instructions to bring the design department up to date and look what happened. You couldn't have done that if you were the man you described back when you were married. Ask Tom about the changes he's seen. He thinks you've been reborn."

"That's very flattering, Michelle. I know I have changed but I wasn't really aware of it as it happened. I think you're right about the twins. They did have a big effect on me. As for the rest and coming here, Tom gave me a challenge and I didn't want to disappoint him."

"Still having a hard time taking credit for your success, aren't you?" she smiled lovingly.

I shrugged. I had to admit I wasn't comfortable with all the praise being heaped on me. It seemed like what I was doing was just common sense. Nothing radical or groundbreaking – just common sense.

Chapter 14
The Wedding

The day of our wedding crept up on me almost without warning. We had made the changes we decided upon at Billy and Carolyn's that weekend. It would be casual dress, held in the pavilion in the park and it would be a civil ceremony. Michelle had carefully contacted her brothers and sons and let them know of the change and why. There was not a complaint or whisper of disappointment. As far as the other guests were concerned, they simply accepted the change and we had no cancellations.

We had discussed having a wedding rehearsal and dinner the day before but chose not to. We had so many guests and family that it would be difficult to organize on short notice. Several of them, my parents included, suggested they had plans already made. Without them, it wouldn't be an appropriate get-together.

Our guests began arriving several days before that special Saturday. My parents had decided to park their motorhome and fly in to Toronto. Their friends picked them up at the airport and brought them to the apartment for a brief reunion.

"Mom, Dad, I'd like you to meet Michelle Gautier, my soon-to-be bride," I said as they came into the apartment. "Michelle, this is my mother Evelyn and my father Stan."

The two women embraced and I could see almost right away that they were relaxed and comfortable with each other. Dad always was pretty easy-going but Mom could be a little distant, as she has been with Sandra. That didn't seem to be the case with Michelle, though.

Their friends were introduced and I spent my time with them, finding out their history with my parents. It dated back to when they were first married and had been neighbours in Vancouver. When a promotion forced a move to Toronto, they were separated but never lost touch with each other. It was something I admired in my parents; friendships that endured over the decades, despite where they lived.

I'm sure they were only intending to spend a few minutes with us but it was almost two hours later that they finally left, taking my parents with them. We would see them again in a couple of days at the wedding and I would have a chance to catch up with them again.

"Your mother and father are very nice, Dex. They seemed to be very happy for us, too," Michelle told me as we closed the door behind them.

"Good," I smiled. "The body language from Mom was much more relaxed than I remember when she was around Sandra. I guess mothers do have the instinct about people after all."

"I don't think you have anything to worry about. If only my mother was half as welcoming," she said wistfully.

"Give it time, love. We'll work on her. She won't be able to resist my charms," I kidded.

"That I can believe," she laughed, wrapping her arms around me and giving me a nice, soft kiss.

Meredith arrived the next afternoon, loaded for bear with two suitcases and a carry-on bag. She too was delighted to meet Michelle as she exited the baggage claim area at the airport.

"It's so good to meet you, Michelle," she bubbled, hugging my fiancée. "Daddy has told me so much about you. He looks so good, too. I was worried after the operation. I thought he might have lost some weight or something. The last time I saw him he was all tanned and fit."

"He's fine now, Merry. I'm so happy it wasn't major surgery. He was back on his feet and back to work the next week. You'd never know he'd been ill."

"I'm great, fit as a fiddle. I need to be to keep up with Michelle," I grinned.

"Yeah … well … you always did have a thing for good looking women, Dad. I never realized my father was a chick magnet."

Michelle burst out laughing as we walked to the parking garage.

"I don't know about him being a chick magnet," she said, "but I have to tell you, the first time I laid eyes on him I thought it couldn't be him I'm supposed to meet. He didn't look anything like a computer nerd. He was handsome and very sexy looking. He got my attention right away."

"I have to admit, my dad is pretty sexy … for an old guy," Merry giggled.

The banter went on and on, usually at my expense as we got to the car and loaded the luggage into the trunk. Our trip to the apartment was reasonably quick; barely twenty-five minutes once we got out of the parking garage. We put all Merry's suitcases in the guest bedroom and gave her some time to freshen up after the long flight.

Later that afternoon, Michelle was in the kitchen starting dinner preparations and it gave me a chance to talk to Merry.

"How are you doing, Merry?"

"I'm fine, Daddy. I have a new boyfriend. Someone I met at work. He's a contractor that specializes in interior renovations. Mostly, older homes. He's very successful."

"That's nice … but is he a good guy?"

"Yes. The next time you're in Vancouver I want you to meet him. I think he's the one. His name is Scott Boyd. He's from Winnipeg, but he says he's never going back," she chuckled. "I think the ocean and the mountains seduced him, and now I hope I've captured him."

I smiled. That was good news, assuming this fellow was right for her. I felt very protective of my daughter, particularly since Sandra and I had separated. She hadn't set a very good example for Merry.

"How is your mother?" I asked, not sure I wanted to know.

"She's better. She has a good job and she's enjoying it. I think she's dating someone but she hasn't told me anything about him. She moved out a couple of months ago and has her own apartment now. I think she could see that we both needed our own space."

"I'm glad to hear she's come out of her depression. I was worried there for a while."

"Were you?" she said in surprise. "I didn't think you wanted to know anything about her any more."

"I've got past that, I guess. You can't be married to someone for all those years and not worry about them, even if we are divorced."

She nodded, "I guess. Anyway, she's in a much better mood these days so I figure it's because of some guy. Maybe I'll meet him soon. Oh … and by the way … she knows you're getting married and she asked me to wish you and Michelle the best of good luck. I think she meant it."

It was my turn to smile. It was one of relief as well as pleasure that the bitterness that might have existed between Sandra and me had dissipated.

"You're going to meet some interesting people this weekend. Michelle has two brothers, two sons -- and a father and his girlfriend that you are really going to like. Tom and Wolf will be coming in tomorrow, along with the local people I've met since I came here. It's going to be very informal and, I hope, a lot of fun. If it isn't, it won't be because we didn't try."

"All I care about, Daddy, is that you are happy. It sounds like you are. I can hear it in your voice and I can see it in your smile. I like Michelle from just meeting her. I think she likes me too."

"I'm very lucky to have found her, Merry. Very lucky. In fact, everything that's happened to me since I split with your mother has been good luck. I hope that doesn't sound mean. I don't mean it that way. It's just how things have been. Who would have thought I'd be Vice President and General Manager of this operation in less than a year. I really like the job and it's not going to kill me, either. I can't believe my good fortune."

~~***~~

Tom and Wolf arrived Friday afternoon and we met at the office. I called a quick meeting of our staff just after lunch and introduced them to everyone. Only a handful had met them during the acquisition. Tom said a few words, praising the progress that Trent had made and thanked them all for their contribution. I think that made a lot of friends with the staff.

Later on, we sat in my office and talked.

"I thought John Flannery's office was in the back," Wolf said.

"It was, but I moved it here to be more visible. I wasn't trying to hide. In fact, I wanted to see and be seen as part of the day-to-day operation. John's old office is now the meeting room. It's a much friendlier environment and a good place to take the customers when they visit. I discovered it had a bar and a washroom so that sealed the deal," I laughed.

Tom took on a serious expression. "You know, Dex, I still marvel at what you have accomplished in this past year. I wouldn't have thought it was possible. We spent a little more money getting Trent up to speed than we estimated but it happened so quickly and so painlessly that anything we invested has been paid back in new business already. You can look forward to a handsome bonus at year end," he promised.

"Thank you, Tom, but don't forget, without yours and Wolf's support I wouldn't have been able to get this far this fast. The side benefit is the morale around here is sky high. I've got a proposal from the design department that I want to be able to share with you when it's ready.

"A couple of the bright young people there were listening to an architect who was visiting our office and heard him mention solid modeling for presentation purposes. It's an expensive process, especially if there are changes to be made. Usually, it isn't done until the final drawings are approved.

"Autocad has a direct-to-laser feature that would allow us to produce model parts in exact scale and in a matter of hours rather than weeks. The proposal is to set up a division that would produce these models at a much-reduced cost and prior to final design approval. It's something we can sell. Anyway, as soon as the proposal is ready, I'll forward it to you along with some projections on cost and return. We're working on this with that architect but he knows it wouldn't be exclusive to him."

I could see the grin on Wolf's face, his brain already calculating how to take advantage of the concept. Tom was nodding, which told me that he wasn't rejecting the idea either. At this stage it was just a proposal and our people had been working on it on their own time. Petra was the originator and she had seconded Miles and Dennis to put the proposal together.

"I like your initiative, Dex. You keep doing what you're doing and this place and Pinecone are going to really thrive. We'd like to take a tour now and meet some of your people personally."

"Let's go," I said, standing.

We started in the administration area and I re-introduced Janice to them, making sure they understood she was the real boss of the operation. They spent several minutes talking with her. Janice introduced our new accounting manager and they welcomed him to Trent personally. I think that made an impression on him.

Rueben and Dick were happy to reacquaint themselves with their new partners and embarrassed me by telling them what a big impact I had on Trent. I knew they were sincere, but still, it was a bit awkward.

Finally, we made it to the design department where I introduced Terry and Petra. Both of them were very enthusiastic about the company's willingness to invest in their department and again gave me the credit for making it all happen. I let them know quickly that Tom and Wolf were the guys who had the last word on expenditures and it was them they should thank.

Wolf took Petra aside and quizzed her about the modeling project. I could see the look of surprise that I had told him about her suggestion but she quickly recovered and began to explain her thinking and what she had learned from the young architect that had originally fostered the idea. Again, she had Wolf's undivided attention.

The tour was over and Tom and Wolf retired to the Rossmoor Suites. They invited Michelle and me to dinner but I begged off explaining we needed to relax a bit before tomorrow and the wedding and reception. They understood and shook my hand, assuring me they would be at the pavilion on time for the ceremony.

When I got back to the apartment, Michelle informed me that all of her sons and brothers and their families had checked in and were ensconced in their hotel rooms. Apparently, all of them were getting together for a family dinner that night. They tried to convince Michelle to have us come along as well but she wisely declined.

Saturday dawned grey and cool and I wondered about the wisdom of the open pavilion at this time of year. Fortunately, by noon much of the cloud had broken up and we would have a mostly sunny and seasonably warm afternoon. The guests began arriving a half-hour before the two o'clock ceremony and Michelle and I attempted to greet them all individually.

I was busy talking to Michael and his wife when out of the corner of my eye I spotted something that completely distracted me. I turned and looked and I'm sure my jaw dropped as I stared in wonder at … the twins!

"Oh my God!" I said aloud.

Michelle was quickly at my side. "Don't be alarmed, darling. This was my idea," she said smiling.

"Dex!" one of them squealed as they both rushed toward me. I assumed it was Adi and I was right.

"Adi … Kat … I didn't expect you," I said in surprise. "How wonderful that you came. It's so good to see you both again." I was embracing both of them as they returned the gesture with enthusiasm.

"How did you get here?" I asked, knowing immediately it was a stupid question.

"We came yesterday. We could not fail to be at our Dex's wedding. When your Michelle telephoned, we told her we would come and here we are," Adi grinned.

"Where is your bride?" Kat asked, looking around.

"Right here," Michelle answered, appearing at my side to greet the two visitors. "I'm so glad you could come. You've been so important to Dex and I wanted to surprise him. It looks like I have," she said, checking the stunned look on my face once more.

"This is amazing. How did you find them?" I asked Michelle.

"You said you both used Skype so I checked and sure enough they were listed and I called them. We had a very nice conversation about you, Dex. The girls let me in on all your secrets, of course."

"Oh oh. I don't like the sound of that," I said with what I hoped was a bit of humour.

"On the contrary, they were very complimentary about your … talents," she smirked.

I turned back to the twins, hoping to divert this conversation before it got out of hand.

"I am so glad you came. It's wonderful to see you again. What are you doing these days?"

"I am soon on my way to Aruba. Another project for ABN-Amro. I think this will be my last one. Kat has a boyfriend and I think if she is away too long, she might lose him. She is going back to Utrecht next week."

"And what about you, Adi?" I asked. "Anyone on the horizon?"

"Not yet," she answered coyly. "I am very … what is the word … particular? I have been spoiled so I will not be happy with just an ordinary man," she laughed.

"Well, I wish you both the best of luck and thank you for being here today. You've made it very special for Michelle and me."

"You could never stop us, Dex. You are too important to Kat and me. Thank you, Michelle, for letting us be here today," she said, hugging my lady closely. Then, both of them kissed me on the cheek and went off to meet the other guests.

"Wow, that really was a surprise," I said to Michelle.

"I'm glad you thought so. They are delightful ladies and they are very grateful to you for what you did for them."

That seemed an odd thing for her to say. "What do you mean?"

"We had a long talk about you one day. Adi and Kat say that you convinced them that they were beautiful when they didn't think they were. You didn't do it by telling them that as much as how you treated them every hour of every day. You behaved just like the Dex I know. I know they were your lovers but it meant just as much to them as it did to you. Today, they have confidence in themselves and that's a tribute to you."

I just shook my head. I felt like I was being given more credit than I was entitled to. "Look at them, Michelle. They are beautiful. Maybe not like a model or a movie star but they are beautiful women. I hope you aren't jealous. You are a beautiful woman too."

"No, Dex. I'm not jealous of them. I'm marrying you, not them. I know your heart. I don't need reassurance. But those two were important to you at the time, just as you were important to them too. They helped you change your attitude and your outlook. They got you on the road to becoming a different Dexter McLeod. The one I fell in love with," she smiled lovingly.

The ceremony started ten minutes late due to the loose organization of the pavilion. It didn't matter. It was conducted by the local United Church minister and all I had to do was repeat the words he gave me and it was over. I turned to Michelle and kissed her to the applause and cheers of the audience. It was a larger group than I realized and it was a happy one as well.

As I slipped the wedding band on her finger, I looked up at her and knew this was the wisest thing I had ever done. We were so right for each other and I think everyone there could see that. I paid the minister and left a healthy donation to his church as a thank you.

We formed a reception line and it was long and moving slowly. Luckily, the caterers were ready and began to set out the food and drink and that kept everyone happy.

I got to meet everyone except Margaret, Michelle's mother. I was disappointed that she chose not to come. I know that Michael had pleaded with her but that apparently wasn't enough. He told me that he thought she might have come if it were a traditional service in a church but the service we chose was anything but. He reassured me that our more casual and open ceremony was delightful and if only his mother objected then it wasn't a failure.

I met all the family members and had a chance to talk to all of them. Michelle's sons were very pleasant and congratulatory. They were pleased that their mother had found someone after the untimely death of their father. I met brother Mark and his partner, Philip. Again, I was genuinely welcomed to the family.

An hour or so later, I was scanning the reception to see if there was anyone I hadn't talked to. I noticed Adi and Wolf deep in conversation, being very touchy-feely with each other. Wolf was my age and had been a confirmed bachelor. On the other hand, he was very skilled with the ladies and I wondered if I should warn Adi. I decided not to. Perhaps there was a spark there that might change things for both of them.

Billy and Carolyn were having a great time, socializing with the family and the guests. I had invited most of the office staff, including Janice and her husband. I had a chance to talk to him and he was an interesting man, running a small sporting goods company. I wasn't surprised that he and Janice had been married for over thirty years. They both looked very comfortable together.

I think the twins met almost everyone since they were the most intriguing guests. Their Dutch accents and formidable appearance caught every man's attention, and most of the women, I suspected. Apparently they weren't bashful about telling how we had met and I wondered just what some of my new relatives would think about that. Oh well, over to you, Michelle. You straighten it out.

Merry spent quite a bit of time with Michelle's sons, since they were the closest in age to her. Carter flew in from Calgary and Kyle from Montgomery, Alabama. I'm sure they were comparing notes on all sorts of things. As I watched, I was sorry Jon couldn't be here but it was a very long trip from northern Chile to Toronto. Money wasn't the issue, it was just that he had only gotten started on this job and hadn't earned any time off. He had promised to come and see us as soon as he could.

I spotted Miles and Rosalind and went over to say hello properly to them. She looked terrific and I could see the look on Miles's face that told me he was smitten. Just a fluke that they met at the picnic but now it seemed to be something more and I was very happy for a very nice young woman.

We promised the twins that we would come to their weddings when they happened. Both of them seemed to think that it wouldn't be too far in the future. For their sakes, I hoped that was so.

Michelle and I stayed to the very end until the last of the guests departed. Among the last to leave the reception were my parents who couldn't say enough good things about the wedding and our new friends and family. I'm sure my father would have loved to have learned more about the twins but I doubt mother would have approved. We would have a late brunch tomorrow morning at the hotel where Michelle's family was staying. A baker's dozen of us would get together once more before we all headed to our respective homes.

We were tired but not so tired that we didn't celebrate this wonderful day in the most intimate manner. It was a warm, slow, comforting lovemaking that we enjoyed that evening, finally drifting off in each other's arms. For me, it was a dreamless sleep. The ghosts of the past were gone and my mind was clear of any doubts. I had found someone to love and who loved me in return.

We drove Meredith to the airport Sunday afternoon, kissing her goodbye with a promise that we would see her soon, either in Vancouver or here in Toronto. Apparently, she was planning to return to attend a trade show early next year that would bring her up to date on the latest in trends for interior design.

Michelle and I were scheduled out on a flight to Miami two days hence. We were taking a ten-day cruise in the Caribbean and naturally one of the stops would be Sint Maarten. We would have enough time in port to rent a scooter and visit the various spots I frequented so I put that on our agenda. The south of France would have to wait a little longer.

As I reflected on my good fortune in the recent past, I wondered how it all came about so seamlessly. Was it my turn? The devastating blow of Sandra's infidelity and greed had prompted me to act in a manner that I was unaccustomed to.

Michelle was right. I had changed and it was a change for the better. I was a great deal more confident. Why not? First the twins, then Tom & Wolf's belief in my abilities. And when a beautiful, desirable woman tells you that it's you she wants, wouldn't you feel confident?

Michelle was beside me, not just physically, but emotionally and, in fact, in our business. She was participating and making my life so much better than I had a right to expect. She had suffered a deeply wounding blow with the death of her husband but, like me, she found a new life. I planned to make sure that she never for a moment thought it wasn't a better life.

The End

Here is a sample from another story you may enjoy:

LEE NORTH

Forgetting
the
Shared Wife

Erotic Romance

We were married in a small church in the suburbs that had time available the following April. I met Judy's family for the first time and I have to say, they were pretty cool toward me. I wondered why, but Judy dismissed my concerns. My folks were in good spirits and welcomed Judy to the family. But again, her parents didn't seem to warm to my folks either. On the other hand, Judy seemed to be quite friendly with Mike. Perhaps because he was a professional athlete or maybe they just hit it off. At least it took some of the pressure off during the reception.

We went on a short honeymoon to Victoria and Seattle before coming home and settling down in our rented apartment. I was working hard to do well in my new sales job and so far, my boss was happy with my results. I had some objectives to reach this year and by mid-year, I was pretty sure I was going to achieve them.

Judy was happy to continue working in the lab. Her hours were more predictable than mine; seven-thirty am to four pm. Mine were irregular, often spending four or more hours on the road traveling from customer to customer, arriving home after six pm after battling heavy commuter traffic.

Life went along quite smoothly for us. We finally saved enough money to put a down payment on a townhouse in the suburbs and celebrated our third anniversary a week after we moved in. This would be our stepping-stone to a proper home someday in the future.

We talked about starting a family, but Judy was adamant that she didn't want to do that until we were more financially secure. She never was able to articulate just when that would be, but since we were both young, not yet twenty-five, there was no panic.

As with any marriage, things tended to slow down a bit in the sex department. Before we were married, we were having sex four or five times a week, except when she was having her period. That dropped to three times weekly after the first three years, and then as time went by, we were down to once or twice a week. When you're working as hard as

I was, you don't notice these things right away, but after a while I did, and mentioned it to Judy.

"Judy, we don't seem to be making love as often as we used to. Is there any reason for that?" I started the conversation after supper one night when we were just sitting quietly on the back balcony of the townhouse.

"No. Why would there be?" The way she answered sounded strange to me. I suppose defensive, but a bit aggressive too.

"I don't know. We used to get together at least three times a week, but not lately."

"Well, we're both working hard and after all, you can't expect us to be full of energy every night." Again, I got that slightly aggressive tone.

"I suppose. But I do miss it. Making love to you is something I really enjoy." I was trying to make it sound inviting to her.

"You'll just have to get used to enjoying it a little less often for now. I'm not always in the mood, you know." I wasn't getting a very sympathetic hearing. I decided in the interests of peace that I wouldn't pursue the matter any further that night. But, it would get revisited.

If you enjoyed this sample then look for **Forgetting The Shared Wife.**

Here is a preview of another book you may also enjoy:

THE MIND TALKER ROMANCE SERIES

AWARENESS
BOOK 1

DARLA DUNBAR

"So sexy…"

"God I'd love to do her…"

"I wonder if I could find that outfit in my size…"

Ananda had to fight laughter, curling an errant lock of dark auburn hair around her finger as she fought through the crowd of people around her. Laughing for no reason, at least none that could be seen by the general population, is typically frowned upon and usually makes finding friends much more difficult. This she had learned the hard way thanks to the cruelty of middle school students and their need to be popular. Still, it never ceased to surprise her how many inane thoughts humans regularly had running through their minds. Sometimes Ananda had to totally isolate herself in order to get a moment's rest, particularly when surrounded by the chatter from all directions. Her honey-colored eyes flitted back and forth as she scanned the mass of people around her, thoughts flying into her mind in rapid succession.

It wasn't like Ananda couldn't turn it off, her ability to hear other people's thoughts. When she was younger, it was definitely more difficult to sift through the roiling voices and images that seemed to seep into her head with little direction or effort. At first when her ability manifested at the tender age of eleven, Ananda was terrified as were her parents, who were ignorant of such abilities. Her older brother, Ryan, had been a source of strength and stability for her as the family went from one psychologist to another attempting to find a reason or cure for the 'voices' Ananda claimed to hear. It was he who helped her find a center in order to control the flow of voices until they were barely more than a brush against her mind. Ryan's move across the country for school was rough though manageable for Ananda as she began to explore the range of her ability and discover the fun she could have with it. Her moral compass wasn't as low as some, so she didn't use it for anything that would get her ahead academically, but she did use it to benefit herself and those she loved.

"Ananda, over here!"

Refocusing on the crowd around her, Ananda spotted one of the few people she could actually call a friend. Kerri wasn't what anyone would call quiet. Her small stature and pixie-like features made it seem as if she could be blown away by a single puff of air, but her exuberant personality and sharp, sometimes biting, use of sarcasm made her seem larger than her thin frame. Bright red hair the color of the sunset and eyes that seemed to change color depending on her mood completed the full package that was Kerri Donahue. However, it wasn't just Kerri's larger-than-life personality that drew Ananda in, it was more of what Kerri didn't exude. Her mind was quiet.

No matter how intently Ananda poked and prodded, she could only get a faint hum and vague feelings from her friend's mind. Rather than being unnerved by that, Ananda felt a sense of relief at finally finding one person who didn't give her a headache just by being around so often. Even with her brother Ryan, Ananda had to occasionally leave in order to calm her own mind and get some relief from his mind's 'voice.'

The fact that Kerri seemed oblivious to how special she was sometimes made Ananda pause and wonder if she was the only one out there with a strange ability. Was there someone out there like Professor X who was searching for people like her? Was there a way to find others? Or did she spend way too much time reading comic books and hoping that some parts of those stories were influenced by actual facts?

In the nine years since Ananda discovered her ability to read minds, not once had she ever come across anyone who seemed to be able to do the same. She had tried going to palm readers and calling so-called psychics, but so far they had all been scams. Their own minds would betray their lack of abilities sometimes before Ananda had even handed over her money. She had decided upon going to NYU with the vague hope that in a city as crowded as New York, there would be at least one other person who shared in her ability that she could commiserate with.

After two years of hoping and searching, she had grown discouraged and until meeting Kerri, Ananda had even considered moving back home to Phoenix and abandoning her search altogether. Meeting the other girl had been soothing to her soul and Ananda felt renewed enough to continue her search for others like her; she had even decided to expand her search overseas.

If you enjoyed this other sample, then look for:
Awareness by Darla Dunbar.

Also by this Author:

<u>Forgetting the Shared Wife</u>

From the Author

If you enjoyed any of my books then please share the love and promote my books in Amazon.

If you write me a review and send me an email I will send you a free book, or many.
(Just know that these emails are filtered by my publisher.)

Good news is always welcome.

One Last Thing, For Kindle Readers...

When you turn the page, Kindle will give you the opportunity to rate this book and share your thoughts on Facebook and Twitter. If you enjoyed my writings, would you please take a few seconds to let your friends know about it? Because... when they enjoy they will be grateful to you and so will I.

Thank You!

Lee North
lee_north@awesomeauthors.org

About the Author

Born in 1940, Lee North is a Canadian who moved to Vancouver with his parents in 1950. His father was a newspaperman and artist. He married his high school sweetheart, and they are blessed with two sons, who then blessed them with four grandsons.

Lee North began his career in wholesale building materials. Ten years later, he got a job at a packaging manufacturer in Vancouver, selling paper and plastic. With hard work, he then became the General Manager. He retired in 2001.

In 2008, Lee North and his family moved to Comox Valley, their paradise valley. He loves traveling. During work years, he widely traveled in North America. And since 1995, through Europe and parts of Middle East.

"I took up writing ten years ago, as a hobby. I had a secret wish to be a writer and the free websites offered that opportunity. I try to confine my stories to locations that I have visited. The characters are fictional but can loosely be attached to people I have met along the way."